DEAD
FUNNY

Tanya Landman is the author of many books for children including *Waking Merlin* and *Merlin's Apprentice*, *The World's Bellybutton* and *The Kraken Snores*, and three stories featuring the characters Flotsam and Jetsam. Of *Dead Funny*, the second title in her award-winning Poppy Fields series, Tanya says, "I've always found Hollywood fascinating. How can you know who's telling the truth and who's acting? Who's real and who's fake? It occurred to me that Beverly Hills would make a great backdrop for a murder mystery."

Tanya is also the author of two novels for teenagers: *Apache*, which was shortlisted for the Carnegie Medal and the Booktrust Teenage Fiction Prize, and *The Goldsmith's Daughter*, which was nominated for the Guardian Children's Fiction Prize. Since 1992, Tanya has also been part of Storybox Theatre. She lives with her family in Devon.

You can find out more about Tanya Landman
and her books by visiting her website at
www.tanyalandman.com

Poppy Fields is on the case!

Also by Tanya Landman

For younger readers

For older readers

DEAD

First published 2009 by Walker Books Ltd
87 Vauxhall Walk, London SE11 5HJ

This edition published 2013

2 4 6 8 10 9 7 5 3 1

Text © 2009 Tanya Landman
Cover illustration © 2013 Scott Garrett

The right of Tanya Landman to be identified as author of this
work has been asserted by her in accordance with the
Copyright, Designs and Patents Act 1988

This book has been typeset in Slimbach

Printed and bound in Great Britain by Clays Ltd, St Ives plc

British Library Cataloguing in Publication Data:
a catalogue record for this book is available from the British Library

ISBN 978-1-4063-4442-4

www.walker.co.uk

For Rod "Maestro" Burnett

BIDDY Ford – *otherwise known as Baby Sugarcandy, star of stage and screen – was sick with nerves. She knelt beside the toilet bowl and waited for it to pass. She was always like this before an important occasion – movie premieres, opening nights, concerts. Every public appearance filled her with this awful, gut-churning fear. And today? Well, she couldn't imagine a more important occasion. No wonder she felt queasy.*

The worst of it was over now, she thought: the nausea was subsiding at last. Putting both palms on the rim of the toilet, she began to push herself up.

She didn't hear the soft tread of feet behind her, or see anyone approach. Only when a hand grasped her head and forced it down did she realize that something was terrifyingly wrong…

THE INVISIBLE GIRL

MY name is Poppy Fields. I'm average height, average weight, average build, and I'm invisible.

Not *literally*, of course. I'm not a superhero. It's just that fading into the background is my speciality. At school, I've mastered the art of sitting in the teacher's blind spot – not at the back with the troublemakers, or at the sides where people who haven't done their homework try to sink into the walls, but slap-bang in the middle of the classroom. What you have to do is maintain an expression of polite interest – not too keen, not too bored – and that way the teacher's eyes sort of slide over you as if you're not there.

At weekends I know exactly how to brush my hair

and precisely which clothes to wear to remain unseen. I've got a wardrobe full of uninteresting garments in indeterminate shades of blue and grey that get me through most situations totally unobserved.

It's not because I'm shy, it's because I'm fascinated by other people. My mum says I study their behaviour with the same curiosity that a scientist gives to the inner workings of a termite colony. She's probably right. To pursue my hobby I've learnt to camouflage myself. No one ever notices Poppy Fields.

So when I first set foot on American soil, why did I have the unnerving sensation that someone was watching me?

It had been OK on the flight over. I'd been sandwiched between Mum and my friend Graham right in the middle of this massive aeroplane. For the whole of the journey from England to America I'd stayed nicely anonymous. In fact, I'd avoided attention so success-fully that when I'd edged out to go to the toilet the steward handing out the lunches had tripped over me. The passenger sitting on the other side of Graham had been hit by several flying trays but he hadn't glared at me even though I'd caused the accident. He hadn't registered my existence.

Collecting our suitcases and going through the

no-man's-land of passport control and immigration had been fine.

But then we'd entered the brightly lit arrivals hall. Mum was looking for the person who had come to collect us when I experienced something strange.

Eyes. Looking at me. Staring. I could feel it like the press of fingertips on my skin.

Alarmed, I whipped around, spinning in a full circle to catch whoever was doing it. Yet everyone in the crowded airport seemed busy with their own concerns – noisily greeting friends, or running to catch buses and trains. No one was looking at me. So why were the hairs on the back of my neck standing bolt upright?

"Someone's watching us," I hissed to Graham out of the side of my mouth. "I can feel it."

"That would be physically impossible," he replied, flashing me one of his blink-and-you-miss-it grins. "But I gather that disorientation is a common sign of jet lag. I expect you're suffering from that. The majority of people who fly across more than five time zones do, you know. And we've flown across eight."

"OK." I nodded. I knew that California was eight hours behind London. Graham had explained all about Greenwich Mean Time and the earth's rotation on the way to the airport – he knows about stuff like that – but I still found it peculiar. We'd taken off from Heathrow at ten o'clock in the morning and flown for eleven hours. *Eleven hours!* As far as I was concerned it was bedtime. But although Graham and I were yawning and our eyelids were drooping, everyone in Los Angeles was just having lunch. No wonder I felt weird. Graham was right. That was all it was, I told myself. There was nothing to worry about.

Mum had started waving energetically at a woman clutching a sign with GREEN FIELDS AND FAR AWAY scrawled across it. "That must be Baby Sugarcandy's secretary," she said to us as we made our way towards her. "Sylvia Sharpe. I talked to her on the phone. She's the one who made all the arrangements."

We stopped in front of a solid woman who was wearing a severe dark suit, tightly-laced shoes and heavy black-rimmed glasses. Her hair was scraped back into a ponytail so tight that it pulled her eyebrows up and made her look as though she was unpleasantly surprised by everything she laid eyes on, including us. She reminded me of my PE teacher at school – strict, efficient and completely devoid of soft edges and sympathy.

"You must be Miss Sharpe!" said Mum warmly. "Hi! I'm Lili Fields. It's really nice to meet you."

"I'm glad your plane was on time," Sylvia Sharpe answered crisply, giving Mum a brief, tight-lipped smile. "The car's this way. Follow me, please."

Just as I was beginning to relax into a happy state of invisibility, Sylvia glanced over her shoulder and flashed an unnaturally white set of teeth at me. I'd been reading a new book about body language on the plane and couldn't help noticing that her grin didn't reach her eyes. That's not a real smile, I thought. But then the one I gave in reply wasn't exactly sincere either. How could it be when we'd only just met?

"You must be Poppy," Sylvia Sharpe said briskly as she led us across the arrivals hall towards the exit. "And I guess you're Graham. If you need anything while you're here, you come to me. Burgers, fries, magazines, movies... If you want it, it's yours. Nothing's too much trouble for Miss Sugarcandy's guests."

Graham and I exchanged a quick look. My mind was fuzzy with tiredness but I couldn't help finding this sudden generosity a little strange. We weren't *guests*, after all, we were *employees*, or at least Mum was. Did Americans always make such a fuss over people who came to work for them? And if they did, why didn't Sylvia's words quite match her manner? It was like she was delivering a speech that she hadn't rehearsed often enough to make it sound sincere. Odd, I thought, very odd. I'm going to keep an eye on her.

We were in the States because my mum Lili runs her own landscape gardening business, Green Fields and Far Away. She won a bronze medal at last year's Chelsea Flower Show for outstanding garden design, but she still spends most of her time mowing old ladies' lawns and digging vegetable plots for people who've put their backs out. Then, out of the blue, she'd had a phone call from America and the next thing we knew she was invited to make over the Hollywood estate of Baby Sugarcandy. Mum was dead impressed but I didn't have a clue who Baby Sugarcandy was. I had to look her up on the internet. She turned out to be an actress and singer who'd been part of the Sugarcandies, a British girl band who'd made it big in the States years and years ago. ("Their first single 'Go Baby Go' spent a record number of weeks at number one," Graham informed me on the plane.) The other girls in the group – Lady, Gypsy and Queen – had sunk without trace when the band split, but Baby had gone on to star in several films. ("She won an Oscar in 1989 for her performance in *Shoot Me Dead, Honey*," according to Graham.) She'd now decided that she wanted to be surrounded by an English country garden, even if she did live in the middle of Beverly Hills. The day Sylvia had called I'd come home from school to find Mum exploding with excitement. She'd given me such a violent hug that she'd almost cracked my ribs. "It's my big chance!" she'd yelled. "Who knows where it will lead? I'll be garden designer to the stars! This is where my career takes off!"

Sylvia had told Mum that Miss Sugarcandy was not only paying megabucks for the design, but she was also happy for Mum to bring me along. "She even said you could invite a friend to stop you being bored. I'll be working all day – you'll need someone to keep you company. She's going to pay for our flights and everything. Who do you want to invite?"

"Graham." My answer had been instant.

"Graham?" said Mum. "Are you sure? Don't you want to bring someone a bit more … well … fun?"

But yes, I was absolutely sure. No amount of persuasion would make me change my mind. True, Graham was generally reckoned to be a bit of a geek, but I knew that his nerdy exterior concealed hidden depths. His head was stuffed full of useful information, and he was capable of sudden, surprising bursts of courage. He'd saved my life when we were on holiday in Scotland and we'd been friends ever since. Plus he was perfect company. I didn't have to talk to him unless I wanted to. He could be relied on to get totally immersed in the *Guinness World Records* for hours on end, leaving me the time and space to pursue my favourite hobby of people-watching.

So as soon as the autumn half-term had started

we'd got on the plane, really looking forward to what lay ahead.

But now we'd arrived Mum's excitement was fading and she was looking slightly green with nerves. "I've never done anything this big," she whispered as Graham and I climbed into the back of the huge car. "Oh, Poppy, suppose she doesn't like what I do?" I squeezed Mum's hand reassuringly, watched her climb into the front passenger seat, and then promptly fell asleep.

It was the squeal of brakes that woke me. That, and being flung so hard against the side of the car that I cracked my head on the window. I blinked, wondering for a moment where I was and why Graham was sprawled across my lap. The car had stopped and was skewed sideways across the road about a hundred metres away from a huge pair of wrought-iron gates that had the house name SUGARCANDY HEIGHTS worked into the design. The Sat Nav had been knocked off the windscreen to the floor and the wrong button must have got hit because it was screaming with electronic enthusiasm, "1171 Orangeblossom Boulevard!" Sylvia was scrabbling around in a frenzy trying to find it but the address was repeated five times before she managed to silence the thing.

"What happened?" Mum cried. "Why on earth did you brake?"

"My apologies!" said Sylvia, dabbing beads of sweat from her forehead with a handkerchief. "A raccoon ran across the road and I had to swerve to miss it. Are you kids OK?"

"A raccoon!" I said, looking out at the empty road. "Where?"

"It's gone. Ran into the trees over there. It's fine, though – don't worry – there wasn't a scratch on it."

I was disappointed not to catch a glimpse – I quite like wildlife. "Did you see it, Mum?"

"No," she said, and her voice was tight with nerves. "I wasn't really looking."

"We've plenty of raccoons on the estate. You're sure to see one soon." Sylvia turned and gave me another of her fake smiles before restarting the engine. She pressed some sort of remote control so the gates swung smoothly open and we entered the grounds.

"We're here," Sylvia announced. "Ms Fields, may I present to you Miss Sugarcandy's estate? It eagerly awaits your expert attention." The words were addressed to my mum. But in the rear-view mirror, I noticed that Sylvia Sharpe's eyes were firmly fixed on me.

DRESSED TO KILL

AS we cruised along the drive, winding in dramatic hairpin bends up the hill, I was stunned by the splendour of Baby Sugarcandy's estate. It was vast: an elegant series of terraces linked with flights of broad stone steps. Columns of tall, pointed cypresses were interspersed with strategically placed orange trees and huge cacti in beautifully crafted terracotta pots. It was difficult to see quite how Mum was going to improve on it and she was clearly thinking the same: I could feel waves of anxiety rolling off her. After the third or fourth bend we caught a glimpse of the mansion and even Graham gasped in astonishment. It was amazing: a construction of stone, glass and steel that looked incredibly modern but also seemed to blend so well into the landscape that it might have grown there all by itself.

"What a remarkable piece of design!" enthused Graham. "Who was the architect?"

I didn't hear Sylvia's answer because at that moment something else caught my attention.

A man was sprinting across the terrace nearest to us and then down the steps towards the iron gates two at a time. I was used to seeing joggers – our local park was full of them – but this man clearly wasn't out for exercise. He was dressed in crisp, white trousers, with a scarlet waistcoat and matching carnation that dangled precariously from the buttonhole of a red-and-white striped blazer. A once neatly knotted bow tie was rapidly unravelling, the ends flapping against his shoulder. Thinning grey hair was revealed when he stumbled and his straw hat fell onto the ground. He didn't stop to retrieve it. When he saw our car, he froze for a second. But then he took off once more, his pace increasing even though his gait was lurching and uneven, and he had a hand to his side as if he had a stitch. He was some distance away, but I could hear what his body language was saying as clearly as if he'd shouted the words aloud. He was panicky, desperate. Terrified.

Elbowing Graham in the ribs, I pointed to the

man out of my window and then asked Sylvia, "Who's that?"

The secretary glanced at me in the rear-view mirror and then looked out across the grounds.

"What the...?" she exclaimed, slamming on the brakes again. But by the time the car had come to a halt, the man had slipped through the iron gates just before they clanged shut and disappeared from view.

"Do you know him?" I asked.

"No." Sylvia's smooth forehead creased in a puzzled frown that made her ponytail jerk. She said crossly, "That's most peculiar. Miss Sugarcandy didn't say she was expecting a caller today. I do wish she'd let me know when she changes her plans, it's so difficult to get anything organized otherwise." She shook her head, tutting. "I'll take you all to the house to meet Miss Sugarcandy first," she told Mum as she accelerated up the drive once more. "Then we'll go to the guest wing. You'll need to get some rest, I should think, before you begin work."

Mum didn't answer. By now she had gone very pale. She turned and pulled a face at me and Graham. When Sylvia stopped the car in front of Miss Sugarcandy's spectacular house and got out, Mum whispered, "I hope this isn't a huge mistake. I suppose if she doesn't like my ideas we can always go home again... But then I won't get paid. Oh dear!"

"It will be fine," I said confidently. Even though I was really sleepy, I was excited about meeting Miss Sugarcandy. The prospect of studying a real life celebrity at close quarters was absolutely fascinating.

But my eager anticipation didn't last long.

When we walked into the vast, marbled entrance hall I realized that I wasn't going to get the chance to see the star in action after all. No one was. Ever again.

Baby Sugarcandy lay in a crumpled heap at the foot of a sweeping staircase, and it was very obvious that she was dead.

A FATAL ACCIDENT?

I was the first person to reach the body, closely followed by Graham. Mum had frozen, standing with an open mouth as if emitting a silent scream. Sylvia was also fixed to the spot, but rather than looking upset she seemed annoyed at the interruption to her well-planned timetable.

I'd seen corpses before – there had been a few of those when Graham and I had been on holiday in Scotland – so I wasn't as shocked as Mum. Even so, it was still pretty distressing looking at that poor broken body and I had to take a few deep breaths to steady myself. Half of me just wanted to run straight back to the airport. But the other half was dead nosy. Remembering from television crime shows I'd seen that I shouldn't touch anything, I bent over Baby Sugarcandy for a closer look.

She was old but not very wrinkly. Small – not much taller than me and Graham, I thought – and she'd really taken care of herself. Her fingernails were beautifully manicured, her lips were neatly slicked with lipstick. She wore a long, white silk dress trimmed with a red-and-white striped sash that was tied in a great big bow on her hip. She looked like she was about to walk down a red carpet with a load of photographers clicking away at her. I noticed that the heel of one shoe had snapped and was dangling by a strip of leather from the sole. And the poor woman's neck must have snapped too, I thought: her head was twisted at such a strange angle. It was a deeply disturbing sight. She was like a china doll that had been smashed by a spoilt child: delicate, expensive, fragile and now damaged beyond repair. No amount of superglue would put her back together.

As Graham and I were absorbing the details, Sylvia Sharpe's tightly-laced shoes padded over the marble floor towards us, closely followed by the soft thump of my mum's trainers.

"How awful!" gasped Mum. "Poor, poor thing!"

"Oh no!" Sylvia said. "How appalling! I am so very sorry you've had to see this. Dear, oh dear. What a ghastly accident! I guess she tripped?"

"I suppose so…" I agreed hesitantly.

"I think her heel came adrift," added Graham.

I looked at the staircase. It was certainly steep enough to kill anyone. If her shoe had given way at the top and she'd fallen, she could easily have broken her neck on the way down. Broken all her bones, in fact.

So why didn't I quite believe it?

I took another look at Miss Sugarcandy. She was immaculately dressed, from her dangly diamond earrings to her pedicured feet. But there was something not quite right. What was it?

Her hair's wrong, I thought at last. I remembered the photograph of her that Graham had found in his *Guiness World Records*. Baby Sugarcandy had styled her hair in a beehive, backcombing it, winding it round and piling it on top of her head until it looked like an enormous ice cream. But now it was a mess, squashed and crumpled like a badly-made bird's nest. What's more, it was slightly damp, as if she'd just stepped out of the shower. I sniffed. A faint whiff of bleach was coming from it.

Sylvia had bent down and was now extending a hand towards the corpse. "I'll carry her to her room," she said. "Her daughter Judy will be home soon. I don't want her to be troubled."

"No!" I said sharply. "Don't touch a thing!"

Sylvia looked at me, astonished. "It was an accident, young lady. We can't just leave her here. If Judy sees her mother like this she'll be in therapy for ever."

But it was too late. At that moment, a theatrical sigh of immense weariness was followed by a series of thuds as several heavy bags were dropped on the marble floor.

I turned to see a thirty-something-ish blonde standing amid a pile of designer shopping bags. She was the complete opposite of Sylvia: all lace and glitzy jewellery and heavy make-up. Her heels were scarily high, her bust was thrust forward in a menacing fashion, and she wore so much lipstick that I was surprised she could speak – it looked as though her lips ought to be gummed together. I assumed this was Baby's daughter, Judy. "Sylvia," she said, "take these bags up to my room, would you? And then fix me something long and cool to drink. I'm *exhausted*."

Sylvia didn't move and Judy looked at her with a frown of annoyance. "Didn't you hear me?" she said. "Why are you just standing there?"

"Miss Ford," Sylvia said slowly. "Judy, I—"

"Yes?"

"I'm afraid there's been a terrible accident." Sylvia stepped aside so that Judy could see her mother's body.

Judy's eyes narrowed for a moment as she took the scene in. "Is she dead?"

"I'm afraid so," replied Sylvia.

A strange look passed across Judy's face: it wasn't sorrow, it wasn't shock, it was satisfaction. She tried but failed to smother a smile of pleasure. Her heels clacked across the marble floor as she teetered towards her mother and said, "Oh, for pity's sake!" She looked down at the broken body. "Sylvia, you'd better carry her up to her room. And then I guess you should call a doctor."

"I think it's a little late for that—" Sylvia began.

"I can see that," Judy said waspishly. "But he'll need to sign a death certificate or something, won't he? Go on, pick her up."

"You mustn't!" I protested. "Don't touch anything."

Judy looked at me and her eyes narrowed into snake-like slits. "And who the hell are you?"

"This is Poppy. Her mother, Ms Fields, is doing some work for Miss Sugarcandy, or at least she was…" said Sylvia.

"First I've heard of it," snarled Judy.

Mum stepped in front of me then as if to defend me from the savagery of Judy's glare. I took advantage of it by slipping a hand into Mum's pocket and pulling out her mobile phone.

Then Graham and I edged casually back towards the front door and stepped outside. I dialled 999.

It didn't work.

"You're dialling the wrong number," said Graham. "It's 911 over here. And you probably need the country code too."

So, thankful for Graham's nerdiness once again, I dialled the numbers he told me to and this time got through to the police.

"I'm at Miss Sugarcandy's house," I explained quickly. "And she's dead. It looks like an accident but I don't think it is—"

"Sure, honey," said a crisp voice at the other end. "Now hang up so people in real trouble can get through."

"I'm not joking," I said.

"Yeah, right."

"No, really. It looks like she's fallen down the stairs. Her neck's broken."

The person on the other end sighed and said, "OK, sugar, but you'd better not be kidding. I'll get a car up there right now. Don't touch anything, and don't let anybody leave the premises."

We went back into the house.

Mum was saying quietly, "Surely the authorities ought to be told? In England if there's a sudden death—"

"There'll be no cops," Judy barked.

"But—" said Mum and Sylvia together.

"She had a fall," Judy said firmly. "Anyone can see that. Sylvia, pick her up. And you." She fixed Mum with a fierce look. "Whoever you are and whatever you think you're doing here, you can go right back to wherever you came from."

"I don't think we can actually," I said. "The police say we have to stay here."

"You called the cops?!" shrieked Judy.

"Yes. They're on their way."

As if to back me up, the sound of sirens drifted in through the mansion doors, faintly distant, but growing louder.

"Great!" sneered Judy. "That's all I need. I'm going to my room."

"You can't," I told her. "We've all got to stay exactly where we are until they arrive. We're witnesses, you see."

"Witnesses?" Judy screamed, her face growing as red as her lipstick. She glared at me. "To what? An old lady whose heel snapped? An old lady who took a tumble and broke her own neck?"

"No," I said, swallowing nervously but staring straight back at her. "Witnesses to murder."

WAS IT MURDER?

TEA was the only solution. When the police arrived we were confined to the vast kitchen while they examined the scene of the crime. Baby Sugarcandy's furniture, fixtures and fittings looked like they had been magically transported from an old-fashioned English farmhouse, which was quite a surprise among all that steel and glass. Finding a copper kettle, Mum filled it and set it on the Aga to boil. Judy sat at the long pine table, picking off her scarlet nail polish and looking furious.

Sylvia stood in the middle of the slate-tiled floor, her hands knotting and unknotting themselves, uncertain about what to do with herself.

Graham and I retired to the far corner, where a

warm, floral-scented breeze was blowing through an open window. Perching on high stools by the counter, I opened my body language book, and Graham opened his *Guiness World Records*. Neither of us read a word, there was too much going on for that. But the books were a useful screen to hide behind while we had a hasty, whispered conversation.

"Are you sure she was murdered?" muttered Graham nervously. "It looked like an accident to me. The police won't be amused if you're wrong."

"Her hair was wet," I replied. "And it smelt funny. Like she'd been bleaching it."

"So? Maybe she had," said Graham.

"With that posh dress on?" I said. "I don't think so."

Graham looked perplexed as if the mysteries of hairdressing were utterly beyond his comprehension. "Well, you wear clothes to go to the hairdresser don't you? And if you go to a posh salon you'd wear posh clothes, wouldn't you? I don't think that's necessarily significant."

I considered. I hoped he wasn't right. I mean, I'd only been to a salon once. Most of the time Mum was happy to trim my fringe with a pair of kitchen scissors but she'd made me go and have a proper haircut just before she'd won that prize at the Chelsea Flower

Show. They had basins that you tipped your head back into while someone else washed it. "She was at home, Graham, not the hairdressers."

"She's a star. She might have an army of stylists in the house for all we know. Probably got a whole salon upstairs."

I was beginning to suspect that Graham might be right, in which case I would be arrested for wasting police time. Oh dear. "OK," I said reluctantly. "But why would she have been walking around with wet hair? When I went with my mum we had our hair blow-dried." I shuddered. I'd hated every second of it.

"Perhaps she got interrupted," suggested Graham. "The phone could have rung, or someone could have come to the door…"

"Mmmmm, maybe." I didn't want to let go of my hunch that things weren't right. But I'd had hunches before that had turned out to be mistakes. Fighting a sinking feeling, I shut my eyes and recalled exactly how Baby Sugarcandy had looked. The soggy hair. The diamonds. "That's it!" I hissed. "Got it. I know what was wrong. Even if she'd been in the middle of having her hair washed, surely she would have taken her earrings off first?"

"That would seem to be the logical thing to do," Graham agreed.

At that point the kettle screamed to announce it was boiling and Mum dashed to take it off the heat. She was intercepted by Sylvia, who said with a contorted smile, "You're a guest here. I'll make the tea."

"Oh, I'd rather—" protested Mum.

"I know what you're thinking. It's what all you British assume: Americans can't make proper tea?"

Mum blushed.

"You're forgetting Miss Sugarcandy's English," Sylvia said. And then she corrected herself. "*Was* English. At any rate, she had me well trained. She was fond of her tea. I do know how to make a 'proper cuppa'."

She did too. A few minutes later Sylvia placed two cups next to me and Graham and, with slightly shaking hands, poured in a dash of milk, then the tea: boiling hot, not too strong. Then she dropped in three lumps of sugar each. "Good for shock," she said, patting me awkwardly on the arm before going off to pour tea for Mum. I appreciated the thought but I didn't really need the sugar: I wasn't particularly shocked. Surprised, yes. A little excited, perhaps, but mostly absolutely riveted.

After a long time in which Sylvia and Mum struggled to make polite conversation and Judy maintained a frosty silence, the kitchen door crashed open and a man who looked just like Friar Tuck in a suit walked in. He was so wide around the middle that he reminded me of a toy I'd once had that bounced back upright no matter how hard and how often I pushed it over. But despite his cuddly appearance there was a glint of steel in his eyes that said he wasn't someone to mess with. He was the kind of man who was surprised by nothing, shocked by nothing and amused by nothing. I fervently hoped that my hunch about the murder was right. I didn't fancy feeling his wrath pour down on my head.

He introduced himself as Lieutenant Weinburger, and spoke first to Judy. "I realize this is a difficult time for you Mrs...?" He paused, waiting for Judy to fill in her name.

"Miss," she snapped. "And I've gone back to my mother's surname since my divorce."

"Sugarcandy?" the policeman asked.

"No!" she spat irritably. "That was her stage name. Her real name was Biddy Ford. I'm Judy Ford."

"Miss Ford," he said, "your mother's body has been taken away now. There'll be a full post-mortem, of course, after which we'll know more about what happened."

"Really! All this fuss over a broken heel," said Judy. "Can't you see it was an accident?"

"Maybe it was," the Lieutenant answered calmly.

"But we need to be sure, Miss Ford. I'd like to ask you a few questions, if I may? Would you care to come through to the living-room?" He phrased it as a question, but from the tone of his voice it was clear Judy couldn't refuse. She stood up and followed the lieutenant through the open door. We heard her heels clacking across the floor and a few seconds later she let out a wail of genuine distress. For a moment I thought she was suffering from delayed shock and her mother's death had finally hit her, but then I heard her words.

"My shopping! Where is it? What have you done with it?"

I couldn't hear Lieutenant Weinburger's reply, but Judy's cries of protest rang loudly through the house. "Taken it? But it's mine! Why do you need to look through it?" Another softly spoken sentence from the policeman, then Judy's exclamation, "This is crazy! Absolutely crazy! Why the hell do you need to check on my movements?"

I could hear Lieutenant Weinburger saying something about "routine enquiries" as they moved away into another room. As soon as the door closed behind them the atmosphere in the kitchen instantly relaxed. Mum and Sylvia began to talk about the gardens and what Baby Sugarcandy had planned for them. Which was just as well because Graham and I now discovered that the floral-scented breeze wasn't the only thing wafting in through the open window: we could hear the conversation Lieutenant Weinburger was having with Judy in the room next door.

Once he'd reassured her about the safety and future well-being of her shopping, the policeman began by asking about her mother.

"Did she seem happy to you this morning?"

"What? You surely don't think she killed herself?" said Judy with withering scorn.

"Just answer the question please, Miss Ford. Did your mother seem happy?"

"Yes, as far as I could tell."

"You sure of that? Was anything bothering her?"

"Of course not!" exclaimed Judy. "She had everything, didn't she? Money, a great house, a beautiful wardrobe. What could possibly have been bothering her?"

"That's what I'm asking you," the lieutenant countered. "How long have you lived here, Miss Ford?"

"I was raised here. Left when I was eighteen. But I've been back a year now. Eighteen months. Something like that. I moved in with Mother when my marriage broke up."

"And you rubbed along together OK?" asked the policeman.

"Just fine and dandy."

There was a pause. I could hear the policeman's shoes squeaking as he paced heavily about. Then he said, "You don't work do you, Miss Ford?"

"What has that got to do with anything?" replied Judy rudely.

"I was just wondering who pays for your shopping. You had quite a haul there, you must have been hard at it all day."

"That's none of your business," she snapped.

"Actually it is," the policeman answered smoothly. "Someone dies unexpectedly, we have to look into everything, consider every angle. It's what I draw my pay cheque for."

"I charge my purchases to my mother's account," growled Judy.

"She must have been one generous lady," Lieutenant Weinburger commented. He changed tack. "Did you see anyone when you left the house this morning? Waiting by the gates, say, or walking in the grounds – did you notice anyone who shouldn't be here?"

"No."

"You didn't let anyone in?"

"Of course not!"

Lieutenant Weinburger cleared his throat. Then he said, "I have to ask, ma'am... Baby Sugarcandy was a rich lady, wasn't she?"

"Yes," Judy agreed reluctantly.

"Who gets her fortune now she's gone?"

"I don't know the contents of my mother's will," Judy said coldly. "But I should imagine she's divided everything between me and my brother. That would be the fair thing to do."

"Your brother?"

"Toby. He's away. Somewhere in South America, I believe, saving the rainforests or something. I don't know exactly."

"We'll find him. Thank you, Miss Ford, you've been very helpful." Lieutenant Weinburger brought the interview to a close. But Judy hadn't finished.

"When will I get my shopping back?" she asked.

"As soon as we've verified your movements," he replied. "You can return to the others now, Miss Ford. Would you be good enough to send your mother's secretary to me?"

Judy gave one last, indignant sniff and then we heard her heels clacking out of the room and back across the hall. When she reached the kitchen, she sat down at the table and began to pick off her nail polish again, but I noticed a smile had crept into the corners of her mouth.

Mum didn't even attempt to talk to her. Curling up in an armchair near the Aga, she fell into a doze.

"Arguments over money or property," whispered Graham, "come number five on the list of the most common motives for murder in the USA."

"You think Judy did it?"

"It seems a highly plausible theory, don't you agree?"

"Yes. She's definitely dodgy. But what about that man we saw? Why was he running away? That was very suspicious."

Graham didn't answer. Sylvia had left the room to speak to the lieutenant and now we could hear his voice through the window.

"Welcome, Miss...?"

"Sharpe," she answered. "Sylvia Sharpe. How can I help you, Lieutenant?"

"How long have you been working for Miss Sugar-candy?"

"A little over a year."

"Did you arrive before or after Miss Ford moved back in with her mother?" asked the lieutenant.

"About a month after."

"Uh huh. And how did they get on?"

"Well … fine, really, most of the time … but..." Sylvia ground to a halt.

"Yes?" prompted the policeman.

There was the scrape of chair legs as Sylvia moved

closer to the lieutenant and we had to strain to catch her next words. "Well, strictly between ourselves, Lieutenant, money was getting to be an issue. Judy loves retail therapy – it's virtually impossible to keep her away from the mall. They'd argued about it, but Judy seemed quite unable to stop herself. As a result of which Miss Sugarcandy had just asked me to close the accounts she had at several stores."

"Interesting," murmured Lieutenant Weinburger thoughtfully. "And how had she seemed to you lately?"

"Miss Sugarcandy? To be honest she'd been very tense. These last few weeks she seemed close to the edge: snapping for no reason, bursting into tears. And this morning she was..." Sylvia groped for the right word. "You know, it was almost as if she was scared of something. Or someone."

"Any idea who?"

"I'm afraid not. She didn't confide in me, Lieutenant. I had the impression that it might have been an old flame. There was a letter from England a couple of months ago that seemed to unsettle her, but she didn't divulge the contents to me. I was her employee, not her friend."

"So who did she talk to? She must have been close to someone."

"Her son Toby. He phoned her regularly and they

talked for hours. But no one else. You know, in lots of ways she was a very lonely woman. Many stars are, I believe."

Lieutenant Weinburger grunted. Then he asked Sylvia the same question he'd asked Judy. "Did you see anyone when you left for the airport today? Anyone who shouldn't be here?"

"Not when I left. But when we got back there was a man – a stranger. An intruder! He was running towards the gates. The girl spotted him. I can't imagine how he got in."

"What did he look like?"

Sylvia gave a sketchy description and then apologized. "I'm sorry, I was driving – I only had a brief glance at him. The children are the ones to ask."

"I'll do that, Miss Sharpe. In the meantime, what can you tell me about Miss Sugarcandy's will? Any idea who gets her millions?"

"Judy and Toby I expect."

"Nothing to you?"

Sylvia gave an embarrassed cough. "She paid me very well, Lieutenant. I wouldn't expect her to leave me anything. And now, unfortunately, I'm out of a job."

Lieutenant Weinburger pressed on. "Tell me more about her son, Toby. What do you know about him?"

"Not much. He's some sort of eco-warrior, I think. He's in South America helping to save the rainforest. I've never met him," explained Sylvia.

"These Brits... What are they doing here?"

"Miss Sugarcandy was getting nostalgic in her advancing years. She wanted the estate to be turned into an English country garden. Lili Fields is a landscape gardener. She was invited here to do the design."

"Why did she choose Lili Fields?"

"Oh... Well..." For the first time, Sylvia stumbled over her answer. "Er... I invited them... I mean her. On Miss Sugarcandy's instructions of course. I'm not quite sure why she chose Lili Fields, to be honest. She gave me her contact details and I took it from there."

"Thank you, Miss Sharpe, you've been very helpful. Send the Brits in now."

Sylvia came back and gently shook Mum awake so that we could all be interviewed. I didn't have a chance to say anything about it to Graham, but I wondered why that particular question had ruffled Sylvia's calm, efficient manner so badly.

INTO THE LOUNGE

BABY Sugarcandy's lounge was odd rather than stylish. The floor was covered with yellow-ish slabs of stone. Glass doors opened out onto a terrace, where a blue-tiled square pond reflected sunlight back into the room, sending patterns dancing across the ceiling. The red-and-white striped curtains on either side looked thick enough to stand up by themselves, and there were so many sofas and armchairs upholstered to match the curtains that they reminded me of deckchairs lined up on a beach.

Lieutenant Weinburger asked us to sit down and we did as we were told. I sank into a chair so soft that I felt as if I was being swallowed like a prawn in an anemone.

Stifling yawns, Mum answered all the policeman's questions. No, she hadn't had any direct contact with Baby Sugarcandy; no, she'd never met Sylvia or Judy before today; no, she hadn't seen the raccoon that Sylvia had braked to avoid; and no, she hadn't got a good look at the man running down the steps – she'd been on the wrong side of the car. "Sorry," she said. "I'm not very helpful, am I?"

Lieutenant Weinburger shrugged and smiled. "No problem," he said. Then he turned to me and Graham.

"It was you who called 911, right?" he asked, fastening his steely eyes on me.

I swallowed and nodded.

"Let's see what you said on the phone…" He looked at his notebook to pinpoint my exact words. "'She's dead. It looks like an accident but I don't think it is.'" Lieutenant Weinburger pierced me with a steady gaze. "What made you say that, kid?"

I took a deep breath. "I thought it looked like murder." My voice came out all squeaky. I cleared my throat and tried again. "It was just a feeling, really. Something wasn't right. Her hair was wet for one thing."

"Maybe she was washing it." Lieutenant Weinburger batted my words away with an impatient flick of the wrist.

"With her earrings on?" I asked pointedly.

"So she forgot they were in." He was unimpressed. "It happens, believe me. When you get older you forget what's what. My own mother doesn't know what day of the week it is half the time. So, tell me about this guy you saw. You get a good look at him?"

I shut my eyes and tried to remember. But what flashed through my head was something completely different: an image of the production of *Mary Poppins* Mum had taken me to when I was little. "He looked like an old-fashioned English gentleman," I said. "Like someone off the stage."

"The stage, huh?" The policeman looked from me to Graham with one eyebrow raised. "You like the theatre? Movies? TV? Crime shows?"

I shrugged but didn't answer. I could see him thinking my imagination had been working overtime and it made me really cross.

"What was the guy wearing?" he asked.

I described the man as fully as I could: the white trousers, the waistcoat, the stripy blazer with the flower in its buttonhole.

"Like this?" Lieutenant Weinburger put a plastic evidence bag containing a tattered red carnation into my hands. The stem was broken. Like Baby Sugarcandy's neck, I thought, and my stomach gave a little heave. "My men found it by the gates," he added.

"I think that's the one," I said. "It looked like it was about to fall out. And he was wearing a straw hat. Quite a smart one. That fell off too."

"We've got that. Anything else?"

"A bow tie."

"Colour?"

"Red." I looked at the policeman intently. "And his jacket was red-and-white stripes, exactly the same colours as the sash on Baby Sugarcandy's dress. *And* the curtains, *and* the sofas. *Weird!* What is it with all this red and white?"

"I don't know, kid. You Brits have funny taste, I guess." Lieutenant Weinburger wasn't at all interested in my observations. I could see him thinking that Graham and I were just a pair of over-excitable children. It was really starting to annoy me. "OK, here's what I think happened," he said. "She's washing her hair, setting it, doing whatever she does to get that style of hers in place. The guy comes to the door and rings the bell. Her PA's collecting you from the airport, and her daughter's shopping, so Miss Sugarcandy goes to answer the door herself. She's at the top of the stairs and trips. He hears her fall, panics and runs away. Until we get the pathologist's report we're going to assume it was just the way it looks. An accident."

I bit back the words of protest that tried to leap out of

my mouth. I was sure I was right: I had a hunch the size of the Empire State Building that Baby Sugarcandy had been murdered. But until the police admitted it Graham and I couldn't say or do anything more. Could we?

The interview was over. We stood up and Mum shook Lieutenant Weinburger politely by the hand.

"Go get some sleep," he told her. "I'll bet you all need it."

"Yes," yawned Mum. "We're really jet-lagged."

"You guys staying here?" the policeman asked.

A cloud flitted across Mum's face. "Oh... I don't know," she said uncertainly. "We were supposed to, but now... Maybe we should find a hotel or something."

Sylvia's voice interrupted her. "They were invited by Miss Sugarcandy and they'll stay here, Lieutenant," she said firmly as she crossed the room towards us. "I'll take you to the guest wing now, it's all ready for you. Take as long as you need to get over your journey."

We followed Sylvia through the kitchen and out of the back door into a large paved courtyard that was lined with potted orange trees. Several shiny metal dustbins were tucked behind a low wall.

"The guest wing is just here," Sylvia explained as we crossed to a door diagonally opposite the kitchen. "As you can see, you have your own entrance. I'll leave you a key so you can come and go as you please. I do hope you'll find everything you need. If not, please don't hesitate to give me a call. The telephones by your beds connect straight through to my office."

My mind was racing, but when I saw the guest rooms all thoughts of crime and punishment were driven out of my head. Downstairs the lounge was as big as a tennis court, with a television the size of a cinema screen. A spiral staircase led up to three massive bedrooms, each with their own bathroom. I bagged the one overlooking the courtyard, and Graham took the one next to mine while Mum opted for the one across the landing, which had a view over the grounds. Sylvia, after ensuring that we had everything we could possibly want, marched away.

I had a foaming bubble bath in a tub so vast there was a serious danger of me drowning. I dried myself on a towel so plush it felt as if it had been woven from clouds, then sank into a bed that resembled an enormous pink marshmallow.

Sleep came almost at once. But just before blackness overwhelmed me I wondered how Sylvia had managed to come in so promptly at the end of our interview. No one had called her, after all. Had she been sitting in our place by the open window in the kitchen? And had she heard everything we'd said?

FULL ENGLISH BREAKFAST

I slept solidly for fourteen hours and probably would have carried on sleeping if Mum hadn't woken me up the following morning.

Wafting a glass of freshly-squeezed orange juice under my nose, she said, "Come on Poppy, love. Graham's up and about already. A new day, a new challenge, and all that. The sun's shining."

"What?" I sat up, squinting at her. "You seem very cheerful."

"Sylvia's been here," replied Mum. "She brought us breakfast, see?" She lifted a tray holding a plate of bacon, eggs and sausages and put it on my lap. "A full English," she enthused. "The complete works!

It's enough to put a smile on anyone's face."

I took a sip of juice and asked, "What happens now? Do we have to go home?"

"No," Mum replied. "Apparently we have to stay here as long as the police are investigating. Sylvia says I might as well go ahead and draw up the designs. It will give me something to do, at any rate."

"OK," I said. "So you're going to be busy all day?"

"Yes. But you can help if you like."

I shook my head firmly: plants weren't nearly as interesting as people.

"Well," said Mum. "Sylvia says there's a pool at the far side of the house that you're welcome to use. There's the TV downstairs and she's left a whole stack of DVDs. Or you could explore the grounds..."

"We'll do that," I said.

"No sneaking around, though," warned Mum. "You heard what that policeman said. It was an accident, remember? Don't go sticking your nose in and upsetting people."

"Me?" I said. "As if." I tried to look innocent and Mum went off with a pen and notebook to survey the gardens.

Graham came in to keep me company while I finished my breakfast.

"What do we do first?" he said.

Crunching a piece of crispy bacon I considered the matter. "Swim," I decided. "I like the sound of that pool. And then we'll search the grounds."

"What for? Clues? I would think it's highly improbable that we'd find something that the police have missed."

"They reckon it's an accident." I stuffed a piece of sausage in my mouth. "They probably haven't looked properly. I want to work out how that man got in."

"The one with the blazer?"

"Yes. Of course, he might have sneaked through the gates when Sylvia set off to pick us up."

"She'd have noticed him," said Graham. "His clothes weren't what you might call inconspicuous, were they?"

"OK. So how did he get in then?" I asked.

"Climbed over the wall?" suggested Graham.

"His trousers were spotless. If he'd done that there would have been marks on them. Anyway, he looked too old for that sort of thing." I spread butter thickly on a slice of toast. "Hey, you don't think someone might have let him in, do you?"

"Who?"

"I don't know. Sylvia could have. Or Judy." I took a bite of toast. Spitting crumbs at Graham I said, "Judy's not at all upset about her mother. And Sylvia said they'd been arguing about money. Maybe Judy let him in before she went shopping?"

Graham agreed that it was a distinct possibility. I'd finished eating, so Graham went downstairs and waited while I got dressed. Brushing my hair forward for maximum invisibility, I gathered up my swimming things and made for the door.

To reach the pool we had to cross the courtyard at the back of the house and then walk along an avenue of vines where a few over-ripe bunches of grapes were still hanging just out of reach.

"You wouldn't have thought the Californian climate would be suitable for cultivating an English country garden. It's so warm and dry here," observed Graham. "How will your mother get things to grow in this heat?"

I didn't bother to answer. I wasn't interested in plants. We reached the end of the shaded avenue and there before us was an expanse of terrace, edged on two sides with columns of thin, pointy cypress trees and dotted with potted cacti. In the centre was a lovely circular pool. My heart lifted at the thought of us having it entirely to ourselves but before we stepped out of the shadows something bobbed across the water that made me sigh with irritation.

Judy. Blonde hair brushed up into a hideous pink cap, wearing movie star sunglasses and a glittering gold bikini. In one hand she held a large, purple cocktail and in the other was a glossy magazine. She was lying on the biggest inflatable I'd ever seen – long, bright green and resembling some sort of amphibious reptile. A dinosaur, perhaps. Or a crocodile.

WHO BENEFITS?

WE couldn't go for a swim with Judy in the pool so we went for a walk instead. We explored for a while, but the weather was incredibly hot compared to England. When we found a shaded seat with a view out over the grounds to the city beyond, we slumped into it gratefully. We were sitting there quietly when we heard the heavy tread of Lieutenant Weinburger's feet and saw the gleaming dome of his bald head on the path just below us. He was with another officer, but neither of them had spotted us. Without a word, Graham and I slid further back into the trees so we could remain out of sight.

There was the crackle of a radio, and the lieutenant

had a brief, angry conversation with the person on the other end. Then he turned to his colleague.

"The pathologist's report has just come through," he said. "That kid was right. It was no accident." He didn't sound pleased, but then you wouldn't expect a streetwise cop to relish being proved wrong by a mere kid.

I punched the air silently and grinned with satisfaction.

"Was she pushed?" asked the other policeman.

"No." Lieutenant Weinburger's tone was troubled. "Or at least she didn't die as a result of the fall."

"But her neck was broken, wasn't it?"

Lieutenant Weinburger nodded. "Yeah. But she was already dead when that happened. She died by drowning."

Graham and I looked at each other, mouths agape.

"Drowning?" the other policeman echoed. "But she was fully clothed! How? Where?"

"In her bathroom. The forensic team are up there now. It seems someone held her head under water. That smell of bleach was cleaning fluid. She was drowned in the john."

"The *what*?" I mouthed at Graham.

"It's an American word for toilet," he whispered back.

"Strangest way to kill someone I ever heard of." Lieutenant Weinburger was shaking his head. The two men continued along the path, moving out of earshot.

"How extraordinary!" said Graham. "I've never read about anyone being drowned in a toilet. That would have to top a list of the Most Unusual Murder Methods."

I didn't answer. "Head in the toilet…" I muttered. "Thrown down the stairs…" Some faint bell rang in a distant memory but try as I might I couldn't quite catch what it was. "Right, Graham," I said, rubbing my hands together, "let's consider the MMO." I'd heard the phrase on a TV crime show and was glad to have a chance to use it in real life. "Motive. Means. Opportunity. Who's number one on our list of suspects?"

Graham considered. "The intruder, I suppose," he said at last. "The man who was running away. He was here just before we found Baby's body – he would seem to be the most obvious culprit."

"OK. He had the means and the opportunity all right. But what's his motive?" I asked.

"I have absolutely no idea."

"He looked English, didn't he? I don't think Americans dress like that. He might be someone from Miss Sugarcandy's past – I mean, she was English too. Maybe he had some sort of grudge against her."

"That sounds plausible," agreed Graham.

"Or maybe he was hired to kill her? That would explain how he got in – someone from the inside could have helped him."

"He didn't look like an assassin," objected Graham. "From my understanding of the criminal underworld, I gather hit men don't usually wear flowers in their buttonholes."

"True." I nodded. "Let's forget about him for a moment. What about Sylvia? Do you think she might have had something to do with it? She could have let the man in. Or suppose she killed Baby Sugarcandy before she drove to the airport?"

"No motive." Graham looked at me, frowning. "She said herself she's going to be out of a job. Why would she do it?"

"I don't know. She's odd though – she's been watching me. Watching you, too. I've caught her at it a couple of times. Like she's expecting us to do something. And her smile is really fake."

"This is Hollywood," Graham said. "Everything's fake. I should think most of the women here have had cosmetic surgery and the ones who haven't are probably saving up for it. I gather Botox injections freeze certain areas of the face. If she's had that particular treatment it might explain why her expression seems insincere."

I reconsidered. "Hmmm... Back to Judy, then. She's not exactly grief-stricken. But then if she'd killed her mum, or got someone to do it for her, she'd at least pretend to be upset to cover it up, wouldn't she?"

"That would be the logical course of action," said Graham.

"Suppose it's all to do with money." I began to construct a theory. "I reckon what we have to work out is who benefits from Miss Sugarcandy's death. Who inherits the fortune? Sylvia's out of a well-paid job now so she can't have had anything to do with it, even if she is weird. Whereas Judy... She's going to be rich, isn't she? No wonder she can't stop smiling. And her brother too, I suppose. But he's not even in the country so it can't be him. If the reason for the murder is money, Judy's the one with motive, means *and* opportunity. The *only* one with all three, as far as we know."

"So what do we do now?" asked Graham. "Observe her movements?"

I nodded. "We'll keep an eye on Judy. If we see anything dodgy, we'll tell the police."

But we didn't get a chance to report any suspicious behaviour. The next time we saw Baby Sugarcandy's daughter she was face down in the pool and she was very dead.

STRANGLED WITH SAUSAGES

GRAHAM and I were still sitting in the shade of the trees when there was a scream from somewhere below us, followed by Sylvia's voice yelling, "Help! Somebody! Police! Help! Help!"

Without thinking, we ran towards it and found Sylvia standing at the end of the avenue of vines. The drink in her hand had slopped down her legs and over her tightly-laced shoes. We reached her just as Lieutenant Weinburger came puffing along the avenue towards us.

"I saw him!" Sylvia gabbled. "The guy in the striped jacket! He was right here! I was just taking Judy a drink. He must have come from the pool. He ran when he saw me. I suppose he's got away."

Without a word, Lieutenant Weinburger pushed past Sylvia and headed for the pool.

We followed him, but we weren't prepared for what we found there. Judy's body was floating face down beside the inflatable crocodile, its rubber mouth gaping in a horrible grin as it bobbed beside her. I thought that Judy had been drowned like her mother, but as we got closer I saw that a length of oddly lumpy rope had been pulled tightly around her neck.

I looked at it, and my stomach heaved with disgust. Beside me, Graham bent over and was sick into a potted cactus.

Someone had strangled Judy with a string of plastic sausages.

"Bizarre..." Lieutenant Weinburger's face was folded into a multitude of lines. "This is one crazy murderer."

He was right, I thought. The obvious way – the easy way – to kill Judy would have been to drown her. So why had her killer chosen sausages as the murder weapon? I shook my head as I surveyed the ghastly scene. It might look insane, I thought, but there had to be an explanation. This wasn't some random act of violence – it had been carefully thought out and precisely staged. Something tickled at the back of my memory again: if only I could dig deep enough I'd know why the murderer had used such weird ways of getting rid of his victims. And if I could work that out, then maybe Lieutenant Weinburger would be able to catch the man who had done it before he struck again.

A whole load of police cars with screaming sirens and flashing lights tore down the drive in search of the man in the stripy blazer, but they didn't find him. An army of men in white boiler suits crawled across the grounds minutely examining each square millimetre of earth for clues, while a second army of men did the same to Baby Sugarcandy's house and everything in it, but none of them found anything useful.

After giving her statement to the police, Sylvia ordered in a takeaway lunch. She sat with Mum at the kitchen table while we waited for it to be delivered. Graham and I took up our positions by the open window, and hid ourselves behind our books.

"Did you see the killer?" Sylvia asked Mum. "You were out in the grounds all morning weren't you? Did you catch a glimpse of him?"

"No," said Mum. "I'm not very observant, am I? I never seem to see anything. Not raccoons, not murderers, no one."

There was a pause, and then Sylvia asked her, "Did the police tell you what happened to Miss Sugarcandy?"

"No," Mum replied.

"It was so awful!" exclaimed Sylvia, wringing her hands in distress. "He drowned her – pushed her head down the … the toilet I guess you'd call it. Why? Why would anyone do such a thing? And now this! Strangled with sausages! And with that crocodile grinning next to her – it was such a sight!"

I had the feeling of eyes pressing on my skin again. I sneaked the tiniest of glances over the top of my book, and sure enough caught Sylvia's eyes just darting away from my face.

"She was looking at us again," I whispered to Graham.

"Probably just checking we weren't listening," he replied.

"Or checking that we were," I said. And then a new thought suddenly occurred to me. "She must have known him."

"Who?" said Graham, surprised.

"Judy must have known that man." I looked at Graham. "When we first saw her she was bobbing around in the middle of the pool. If she'd seen a stranger – someone she didn't know – she'd have made a fuss, wouldn't she? She'd have screamed or something. And she'd have stayed in the middle of the pool and he wouldn't have been able to reach her without jumping in. We'd have heard the splash from where we were. But we didn't hear a thing. So she must have gone over to the side to talk to him."

"That seems a sound hypothesis," said Graham. "Maybe she knew him because she *did* get him to kill her mother – perhaps she *did* let him in. Let's suppose she was after the money. But if they were in it together why would he have killed her?"

"Could they have had an argument?" I asked. "We'd have heard that too though, wouldn't we? We were pretty close to the pool. Maybe he planned to kill them both all along. But why? What's his motive? And how did he get in today? Do you think the same person let him in again?"

Graham shrugged but said nothing.

I had the nagging sensation that I'd forgotten something. It was like leaving the house without my homework – I felt there was something missing, something I'd overlooked. But the harder I tried to put my finger on it, the more it slipped through my grasp. Angry and frustrated, I stared at my book until lunch arrived and distracted me.

* * *

We gathered around the table while Sylvia unwrapped paper packages.

"I ordered in fish and chips," she explained. "There's an English couple a few blocks away who do them. Comfort food," she added, putting the contents onto plates. "I figured we could all use some."

"Lovely," Mum said with false cheeriness, sitting down to eat. "Proper big, fat chips! Not like those skinny little fries you Americans seem to prefer."

In response, Sylvia picked one up and looked at it in admiration, before taking an appreciative bite. "Big, fat chips," she echoed. "You're right. That's the way to do it!"

I dropped my knife and fork. I was rigid with shock. As my cutlery clattered to the floor, Sylvia said anxiously, "Are you OK?"

"Say that again!" I hissed.

"Are you OK?" she repeated.

"No. What you said before … about the fries."

"Er… Big fat chips?"

"No. The other thing!"

"Mmmm…" Sylvia took another chip. "That's the way to do it?"

I slammed my hand on the table so hard that the salt and pepper pots leapt into the air.

Graham leant across and stared at me. "What is it?"

he asked. "What does it mean?"

Memories crashed over me like a great wave. Chips. Salt and vinegar. Sand. Seaweed. Rubber rings. Lilos. Ice cream. Kids laughing. Screaming with excitement. Pointing. Red and white stripes. Velvet curtains. And there, high on the little stage, brightly painted puppets. The high-pitched screech of Mr Punch... Dropping his baby in the toilet... Throwing it down the stairs... Hitting Judy... The crocodile eating his sausages... And shouting with every victory, "That's the way to do it!"

I felt the blood drain from my face, and then it seemed to rush back in a sudden gush that made me hot, pink and dizzy. I looked at Graham, my chest tight with excitement. "Punch and Judy," I said breathlessly. "It's all to do with the Punch and Judy show."

"Yes!" Graham punched my arm in triumph. "Of course it is!"

Mum gasped and clapped a hand to her mouth.

"Call Lieutenant Weinburger," I told Sylvia. "We need to tell him right away!"

But trying to convince the streetwise cop wasn't an easy task. He looked from me to Graham and back again, his eyes icy blue pools of disbelief, but I carried on regardless.

"It's a puppet show," I explained. "Mr Punch is the

bad guy but everyone loves him. He chucks the baby in the toilet and then throws it down the stairs. So that's Baby Sugarcandy, you see? Then he does away with Judy and there's a whole bit with a crocodile – like that green inflatable in the pool. I can't remember how it goes, exactly, but I'm pretty sure the crocodile eats his sausages. And then he bashes the policeman."

"He assaults a cop?" Lieutenant Weinburger's tone was acid.

"Erm … yes," I said.

"You guys *like* this show?" asked Lieutenant Weinburger incredulously. "You let *kids* watch it?"

"It's very funny," I said huffily.

"The famous British sense of humour, huh?" the policeman grunted. "Serial homicide inspired by a puppet show? I don't think so—"

"But don't you see?" I demanded crossly. "It all makes sense. It's perfectly logical, to the murderer at any rate. But what we still don't know is *why* he's doing it. There must be some link with Miss Sugarcandy – way back in her past, maybe. Perhaps she once saw the show – or knew someone who performed it? The guy in the jacket – maybe he's a Punch and Judy man! It would explain the red and white stripes."

"A killer puppeteer?" Lieutenant Weinburger said, his eyebrows raised sky high with disbelief. "That's the craziest thing I ever heard. But it's a lead, I guess. We'll have to follow it. I think you kids had better come downtown to the Police Department."

THE PUNCH AND JUDY MURDERS

I was the only person who had got more than a passing glimpse of the killer, so it was me who was stuck in front of the police computer trawling the internet for information about the Punch and Judy show. It took *ages*. There seemed to be hundreds of sites and millions of photographs, and as I examined each one it seemed to get more and more hopeless. The man I'd seen was old. Even if he *had* once been linked with puppets he'd probably retired long ago. We might never find him.

Luckily Graham was there to help me. We'd been searching for two solid hours with no success when Lieutenant Weinburger came in. "Find anything?" he asked.

"Not yet," I sighed. "But we'll keep working on it."

"This is police work, kid," he said drily. "It's one per cent inspiration, ninety-nine per cent perspiration. But I think I can give you a break."

I brightened at once. "Really?"

"Yeah. I've been making some calls; digging into Baby Sugarcandy's past. Biddy Ford, I guess I should call her. It's midnight in England right now – I had to pull a few people out of bed so it took a while. Seems she was married before she became famous. When she was eighteen years old she got hitched to her childhood sweetheart. As soon as the Sugarcandies began to make it big, the band's manager made her ditch him. Said it was marriage or a singing career – she had to make a choice. So she divorced the guy, changed her name to Baby Sugarcandy, and came to the States. When she got into the movies she married an actor, and had the two kids. It didn't last, though. They split a few years later."

"What was this childhood sweetheart called?"

"He went by the name of Len Radstock."

"Type it in, Poppy. Go on," Graham said.

Heart thumping, I entered his name into the search engine. Up came dozens of entries, mostly relating to Radstock, a town near Bath. I scrolled rapidly down through sites about town councillors, schools and shopping facilities. But then – on the fourth page – I found something else. A reference to a newspaper article about the May Fayre in Covent Garden, which seemed to be held every year to celebrate Mr Punch's birthday. There was a list of participants' names and it included Len Radstock. Hardly daring to breathe, I opened the page and found a photograph beside the feature. I clicked to enlarge it. Two dozen men stood in a line, each with a Mr Punch on their right hand. And there on the end was a man in a red-and-white striped blazer. He was unmistakeable.

"That's him," I breathed. "That's the murderer."

Knowing *who* he was didn't solve the problem of *where* he was but it gave the police a starting point. In a slightly irritated fashion, Lieutenant Weinburger told his force about the new lead and where they should direct their attentions. Then he held a press conference to warn the public that a killer puppeteer was on the loose.

Meanwhile, we turned our minds to the question of motive.

"I still don't understand it," Graham said.

"What?"

"Well, what are we saying? The motive isn't money, it's revenge?"

"Looks like it," I agreed.

Graham frowned. "I can see why he might be angry. I understand that nobody welcomes rejection. But why wait until now to do anything about it? It happened years ago!"

I considered. "People do strange things when they get older. I mean, Sylvia said Baby Sugarcandy was getting nostalgic – that's why she wanted to have an English country garden. Maybe Len Radstock had started thinking about the past too, only instead of making him soppy, he became bitter. Maybe he thought she'd wrecked his life. He wanted to punish her for it. Her and her family."

"But," said Graham, "does that still mean it was Judy who let him in?"

"I suppose so. Judy wanted her mother out of the way for the money. I guess Len did the job for her."

"Did she let him in the second time too?" asked Graham.

"Must have done," I replied. "Maybe she'd arranged to pay him. She didn't know he had his own plans for her."

"Hmm, I see." Graham nodded thoughtfully.

It all sounded just about possible, I reckoned.

"Do you think he'll attack anyone else?" asked Graham.

"No idea. She's got a son, hasn't she? The eco-warrior. He might be in danger."

"He's in South America though. He should be safe enough there."

After the press conference, the TV news had run a story about the Punch and Judy murderer. By the time Lieutenant Weinburger drove us back to the estate an army of reporters had gathered outside the entrance. He slowed to a crawl to ease the car through the crowd and ground to a complete halt as we waited for the gates to swing open and let us through. A police officer stepped forward and tapped on the window.

"You might want to talk with this lady, sir. She's from across town. Says she sold a carnation to the old guy." He indicated a stout woman in the crowd with an extraordinarily large flower pinned to her jacket.

She didn't wait for permission to speak. Without warning she launched into her story, her voice loud enough for all the waiting reporters to hear.

"When I saw the picture of that fella on the TV I swear I almost died! I said to my sister, 'That's him! That's the guy I sold a flower to only a coupla days ago.' I remember it well because he said he wanted something real plain and tasteful and I told him, 'Mister, Tasteful is my middle name.' I did just exactly what he told me to: a single bloom with just one piece of greenery. Looked pretty small to me but I gather that's the British taste." She sniffed disapprovingly. "Anyway, he pinned it to his jacket and I have to admit he looked just swell. And that guy was so happy! He was acting like it was his wedding day. How was I to know what he'd do next? When I think of what happened after he left! Gee! If I'd the slightest idea he was homicidal I'd have called the cops right away. Baby Sugarcandy, too! D'you know I was one of her biggest fans? I bought all her records – way back when you could still buy records, now it's all CDs and computer downloads. Lord, but it's hard staying on top of all this new technology. Some days I wonder how I'll manage to keep the store going with people ordering their corsages and wedding bouquets from halfway around the world over the net. I can't figure out why they won't just use the local store where they can choose their own flowers…"

The woman took the smallest of breaths and Lieutenant Weinburger seized his opportunity. "Thank you ma'am. How did the guy pay?"

"Cash. I told my sister—"

"Cash. There's no credit card receipt? Nothing we can use to trace him?"

"Well no, but I thought you'd want to know I'd seen him. My sister said, 'Shirley, get over there and tell the cops right away. They'll be looking for him—'"

"Of course ma'am." Lieutenant Weinburger beckoned over one of his men. "Officer, take this lady's statement. See if she can identify the carnation that we picked up in the grounds." He revved up the engine again to indicate the conversation was at an end. As he drove through the gates, I could hear the lady's story being poured into the ear of the policeman.

"That interview will be ninety-nine per cent perspiration," I muttered to Graham. "Do you think he might have said anything to her about where he's staying?"

"He wouldn't have got a word in edgeways!" replied Graham.

"Are we going to be safe here?" Looking up at the mansion I felt suddenly anxious. Two people had already died there. "Suppose Len Radstock comes back?"

"With armed police crawling all over the grounds?" replied Graham. "Right now I'd estimate that this is probably the safest place in Hollywood."

The car pulled up in front of the house. Mum ran down the steps to meet us.

"Did Poppy help?" she asked Lieutenant Weinburger.

"Yes ma'am," he said. "She provided us with a real neat solution."

He didn't sound exactly thrilled and for the first time I felt a glimmer of sympathy for him. Because as I climbed out of the car I felt the tiniest suspicion tiptoeing across my mind that maybe – just maybe – the solution was a little *too* neat...

THE MASKED INTRUDER

THAT night, when Sylvia cooked us supper in Baby Sugarcandy's kitchen, she seemed more relaxed and at ease. Her hair was still scraped back, but the ponytail wasn't quite so tight. The dark suit had been replaced by a light summer dress, the tightly-laced shoes with a pair of strappy sandals, and there was even a slick of lipstick across her mouth. It had been badly applied, as if she wasn't used to wearing it, and traces of red had got on to her front teeth, making her look as though she'd been eating raw liver.

But she was smiling in an almost sincere way when she said to me, "It's just as well you were here to help the police! It's only a matter of time before they catch the guy now." She started frying some chopped onions. "What a relief that'll be!" It was spoken with real feeling.

"Let's hope the police arrest him before he finds Toby," said Graham gloomily. "Or there might be another nasty murder."

Sylvia added meat to the pan and it sizzled away while she boiled water for the spaghetti. "He can't hide for ever. And then this will be over and we can move on. It's been a rough couple of days! As for Toby – he must be deep in the jungle somewhere. If the police can't find him, an old man like Len Radstock won't be able to. And they're sure to pick him up soon, his picture's been on TV, it's all over the papers – someone's going to recognize him."

Mum began to catch Sylvia's optimistic mood. She moved over to the counter and picked up a block of parmesan cheese. "Want me to grate this?" she asked.

"Sure." Sylvia smiled at her and I noticed again that it was almost, but not quite, genuine. Soon they were absorbed in a conversation involving global politics and I curled up in the armchair near the Aga so I could watch them.

For someone who was about to be out of a job, Sylvia seemed unnaturally cheerful. There was a spring in her step as she tossed salad leaves in dressing. Energy fizzed from her fingertips as she set knives and forks on the table. Electricity positively crackled from every pore as she dished spaghetti into bowls and poured the meaty sauce on top.

"Dinner is served," she announced, pulling a chair out for me and Graham and beckoning us to the table. "Enjoy."

The food was good, and I tucked in. I pretended to be absorbed in the process of eating, but really I was studying Sylvia closely. The secretary didn't give me a second glance and that in itself was odd. She'd been watching me and Graham ever since we'd arrived and her lack of attention now only made it more noticeable. It was like having a radio on in the background – you're only really aware of it once it's switched off. So why had Sylvia been watching us? And, more importantly, why had she stopped? It was as if she'd been desperately hoping we'd do something, and we'd done whatever it was, so she'd lost interest in us.

Mum was laughing at some joke Sylvia had made. She seemed to think Sylvia was OK. And Graham hadn't been bothered by her scrutiny. Why did I have this gut instinct that the secretary couldn't be trusted? Was it those insincere smiles? Had she really had Botox injections? Surely she was too young for that?

I thought back to the day she'd picked us up from

the airport. Of course, I'd missed most of the journey. I'd been fast asleep until she'd braked for that raccoon and the Sat Nav had fallen off and gone bonkers. I wished I'd seen it. She'd said there were loads of raccoons on the estate but we hadn't seen a single one. Maybe I just wasn't looking in the right places. I'd have to remember to ask someone about them.

When the meal was over, I was unable to stop a huge yawn escaping from my mouth. It was catching. Graham yawned too, and then Mum. Stifling it she said to Sylvia, "I think we'll crash now, it's been a long day. Thanks for the meal, it was delicious."

For a moment Sylvia didn't answer. She was looking intently out of the window. I glanced over, but from where I was sitting all I could see in the glass were the reflections from the kitchen. Suddenly, for the first time, a smile that went all the way up to her eyes creased Sylvia's face in two. She concealed it almost at once, turning and saying blandly, "Hey, no problem. I'm glad you enjoyed it." Mum didn't notice her delayed reply, but I did. I saw Sylvia's expression and wondered what had made her so happy that for a split second she'd seemed lit up from within.

I was just drifting off to sleep when a loud clatter from the courtyard below jerked me awake. For a confused moment I didn't know where I was or what was happening. As I sat up and rubbed my eyes there was another bang that sounded suspiciously like a metal dustbin being pushed over.

"Graham?" I called, climbing out of bed and pulling on my dressing gown.

Graham emerged from his room and joined me on the landing. "I heard it too." We looked at each other nervously, then went down the stairs together and approached the front door. I pulled it open and as I peered into the blackness the security lights snapped on.

Beside a toppled dustbin in the corner of the courtyard was a raccoon. It was caught in the sudden glare, sitting on its haunches, a half-eaten slice of pizza grasped guiltily in its front paws. Black markings on its face made it look as though it was wearing a bandit's mask, and its stripy tail was sticking out sideways.

"Little thief!" I was delighted. "See that mask and those stripes? He looks like Burglar Bill. All he needs is a bag with SWAG written on the side!" The creature froze for a moment, dazzled by the bright light. I took a small step forward hoping to get closer but it ran away, clutching its prize in its teeth. I laughed, and then said to Graham, "Our first raccoon! Sylvia said we'd see one." I glanced around, half-expecting the secretary to appear: she must have heard the clattering too.

It was then that I noticed the kitchen door was ajar. Sylvia had said she was going to bed. Why hadn't she locked up?

A cold sliver of fear knifed me between the ribs. I peered harder into the starkly lit courtyard and then stifled a scream of horror.

Behind the toppled dustbin was the unmoving body of Sylvia. A dark stain had pooled on the stone slabs around her head. When we approached we saw that a baseball bat – which looked just like Mr Punch's stick – had been discarded at her feet. A wave of terrible sadness crashed over me, but tears of pity turned to tears of rage when I saw what her attacker had done. It hadn't been enough to kill her: he'd made fun of her too. On Sylvia's head, perched at a mocking, jaunty angle, was an old-fashioned English policeman's helmet.

POLICE PROTECTION

"IT'S a nightmare. I wish we'd never come here. Why did I take this job? I want to go home!"

Lurking in the shadows at the top of the spiral staircase I could hear Mum's wailing quite clearly but Lieutenant Weinburger's reply was harder to catch.

"I appreciate your feelings, ma'am, really I do, but it's just not possible for you to leave at the moment," he said. "Your daughter is the only witness we have. We'll need her to identify Len Radstock when we arrest him."

"*If* you arrest him!" Mum snapped accusingly. "All those police in the grounds and he still managed to slip through! And the whole time we were having that meal with Sylvia he must have been out there, looking in at us… It's horrible!"

I couldn't control the violent shudder that seized me at the thought of Len Radstock watching while we ate spaghetti; waiting, while we crossed the courtyard to the guest wing. Had he been out there in the shadows all the time? Had he watched me and Graham discover Sylvia's body? How close had we come to being his next victims? Where was he now?

It was very late and Mum had insisted that Graham and I go to bed and get some sleep while the police did what they needed to do at the scene of the crime. We'd been despatched upstairs with a comforting cup of hot chocolate. Mine was now stone cold on the bedside table. Sleep was utterly impossible. When Lieutenant Weinburger had knocked discreetly on the front door to interview us, I'd gone downstairs to open it, only to be bundled back up to my bedroom by Mum. "She's not getting involved in any more of this. It will give her bad dreams for life!"

I'd faked obedience, climbing into bed and pretending to sleep. When Mum had finally gone back down to talk to the policeman I crept to the top of the stairs to eavesdrop. Graham was already there listening in.

"Why Sylvia?" lamented Mum. "Why kill her? It's

not like she was even related to the others."

It was the question that I wanted to ask, and I bent forward to hear the lieutenant's answer.

"He seems to be targeting anyone closely connected with Baby Sugarcandy," he said slowly.

Mum's voice rose an octave. "So we're in danger too?"

"I'm afraid we have to consider it as a possibility ma'am. I've stationed officers all around the perimeter of the estate. No one can get through now, believe me."

There was a pause, and from the rustle of tissues I could tell that Mum was crying. Lieutenant Weinburger let her be for a while, and then asked, "How much did you talk to Sylvia?"

"Not much. It was just polite stuff. Nothing important," snuffled Mum.

"She didn't mention a boyfriend?"

"No," replied Mum, confused. "Why?"

"We believe she was planning on getting married," said Lieutenant Weinburger.

"Really?" Surprise dried up Mum's tears. "I had no idea."

"I was checking over her room. She had a whole file of cuttings and leaflets about wedding venues, caterers, that kind of thing. They were spread out on her bed.

Looked like she was planning something real big."

"She must have bagged herself a millionaire." Mum blew her nose.

"She never mentioned anything to you?"

"No, but I'd only known her a couple of days or so. Poor Sylvia! That's so sad." Mum was off again, weeping into a fresh tissue.

My mind was alive with questions. Sylvia had seemed so cheerful this evening – was it because she was excited about getting married? The words of the florist echoed in my ears: "That guy was just so happy! He was acting like it was his own wedding day." Could there be a connection? And if Len had been looking so happy when he bought the buttonhole why did he look so scared when I saw him later? I was distracted from this line of thought by Lieutenant Weinburger.

"I found this in her room too," he was saying. "I thought you'd appreciate having it back."

"Oh." Mum sounded puzzled, and I edged forward to see what he'd given her. "I wonder how she got hold of this?"

"You didn't send it to her?"

"No."

I twisted my head, pressing it against the banisters, craning to see what Mum was holding. It was a photograph. I couldn't see who was in it but Mum was saying, "It was taken at the Chelsea Flower Show last year. I won a bronze medal."

I remembered it well. Mum had clamped a restraining arm around my shoulder and forced me to be in the press photograph despite my protests.

"I guess Sylvia ordered a copy from the newspaper," said Mum. "She must have wanted to be able to recognize us at the airport. Look at Poppy's expression! She hates having her picture taken. That scowl could crack a camera." Mum lifted the photograph up for closer inspection. "That's odd," she said.

"What?" asked Lieutenant Weinburger.

"There, look. Can you see? Sylvia's scribbled on it. I wonder why she drew a circle around Poppy's head?"

"Just doodling, ma'am. Probably did it without thinking."

I wasn't so sure. Sylvia had been watching me from the very beginning. The fact that she'd circled my face in the photograph struck me as being both sinister and significant, although I had no idea why.

Downstairs, the adults carried on talking a while longer, but they didn't say anything else that was of interest to me or Graham. When the policeman got off the sofa to go, we took ourselves quietly back to our rooms, climbed into our beds and faked deep slumber.

I found that real sleep was slow to come and when it finally arrived it was full of horrible dreams. I woke at dawn, snapping out of a nightmare in which I was being chased by a giant raccoon, whose red lips were spread in a grin, and who cackled madly like Mr Punch.

THE ECO-WARRIOR

I had a deep, foaming bath and lay soaking in it until my fingers and toes were as wrinkled as raisins. Climbing out, I dried myself, feeling tired before the day had even begun. Mum would be pale with misery, fretting about Sylvia, terrified about the wandering murderer and the likelihood that we were next on his list, and wailing every five minutes that she wanted to go home. I found the prospect of coping with her feelings quite exhausting.

But by the time I went down for breakfast, it was nearly lunchtime and Mum's anxieties seemed to have vanished. Baby Sugarcandy's son Toby had finally arrived and his presence had wiped everything else from her mind.

He was Indiana Jones, Robin Hood, Dr Who and Superman all rolled into one, and from the amount of frantic hair flicking going on I could tell that Mum had fallen for him Big Time. Even Graham was listening with keen interest to everything he had to say. I could quite understand. When I walked down the staircase and came face-to-face with Toby I felt my knees going strangely weak and I had to quickly sink into the sofa. He was spectacularly handsome, but ruffled around the edges as if life had bumped him about a bit. I could see in one glance that he'd had adventures, done brave things, travelled round the world setting it to rights. He was earthy, rugged and real, and his eyes exuded as much welcoming warmth as a bowl of melted chocolate.

"You must be Poppy. Lieutenant Weinburger told me about you. You're one smart cookie."

I flushed scarlet to the roots of my hair. I didn't confess to the raccoon nightmare, or to the fact that I'd lain awake for hours terrified that Len Radstock was on his way to get me. Instead I smiled and asked, "When did you arrive?"

"I flew in to LA late last night and stayed in the airport hotel. Figured it was best not to disturb you all up here. Of course, I didn't know then that you'd be awake in any case. I guess you didn't get much sleep, huh?"

I shook my head.

"I'm sorry you guys have had such a tough time," he told us. "It's an ugly thing to have got involved in. I bet you can't wait to get back to England."

"Oh, it hasn't been so bad," said Mum, tossing her hair across her shoulder. "The police have been very kind. And we can't leave until the murderer's caught." She gave a little cough and then said, "I'm so sorry about your mother."

"Yeah, me too. She was one great lady. I'm going to miss her." He spoke the words with a quiet dignity, but there was no doubting the depth of his grief, and my heart pounded in sympathy. He was the first person to be genuinely upset by Baby Sugarcandy's death. I felt tears pricking my eyes and Graham looked choked too.

"I feel so bad," he murmured. "I knew she was scared. She told me on the phone that an old flame was bothering her – sending her letters, calling her at night. I thought he was just some harmless guy, you know? If I'd taken it more seriously she and Judy would still be alive."

"You can't blame yourself," said Mum. "The man's mad. No one could have predicted what he'd do. Or what he might do next," she added fearfully.

"I guess not," Toby conceded. "But I feel guilty as hell. If I'd been here, I could have protected her, protected them both. And now Sylvia – some woman I never even met – killed just for working here! It's terrible." He rubbed his forehead as if he was developing a headache and there was silence while me, Mum and Graham all looked at each other wondering what to say. In the end it was Toby who spoke first. "Sorry guys, I didn't mean to dump that on you. Let's talk about something else! Lili, you came here to look at the grounds, didn't you?"

"Yes, your mother wanted an English country garden. I'd started working on some designs. But I suppose you won't be needing them now..."

"Mind if I see them?"

"Of course not!" Talking about gardens was Mum's favourite occupation. She fetched her sketchbook and opened it on the table.

Toby began leafing through her drawings and plans.

"I thought the copse at the top could be turned into a bluebell wood," said Mum. "It would be beautiful in spring. Then maybe a wildflower meadow below it, and something more formal around the house – a pattern of box hedges immediately in front and then a long herbaceous border backed by yew hedging, and perhaps some old-fashioned roses? Climbers would be lovely up against the walls with some honeysuckle too. The smell would be heavenly in the summer."

"Sounds great!" Toby nodded and looked at her thoughtfully. "You're one talented lady," he added. "You know, an English country garden would be a fitting memorial to my mother – a kind of tribute to her. Sentimental of me, I guess, but I'd like her to have what she wanted. Heck, it's all I can do for her now. Will you carry on and finish the designs for her? For me?"

Mum was utterly thrilled. She flashed him a smile so warm it could have melted the ice caps. "Of course I will. It will be a pleasure," she said eagerly. Then she frowned. "There's only one problem."

"What is it?"

"Well, the climate here's so hot and dry. We'd need to put in some kind of irrigation system. It would be terribly expensive."

"Money's no problem!" Toby replied firmly. His hands closed over Mum's. "Let's have a coffee. Then you can show me around the grounds. I'd love to see exactly what you've got in mind."

"I think I'll go for a swim now," I said loudly. "Are you coming, Graham?"

Graham hesitated, but I gave him such an intense glare that he took the hint and scurried away to collect his trunks. I was feeling suddenly uncomfortable, and wasn't entirely sure why. The sight of grown-ups ogling each other was always stomach churning but there was more to it than that. Leaving Mum to talk about planting plans with Toby, I grabbed my things and took Graham with me for a good, long think.

We couldn't cross the courtyard – it was full of police crawling over the flagstones looking for hairs, bits of fabric, anything that might help in the case against Len Radstock. Instead we edged around the guest wing and along the front of the house. From here we could see the grounds spread out below us. They were lovely, I thought, just right for the dry heat of California. There was something excessively lavish about the idea of transforming it all into a soggy, damp corner of England.

"Why didn't Baby Sugarcandy just move back to Britain if she wanted an English garden?" I said crossly.

"What?" said Graham.

"All this irrigation and stuff Mum's planning... It doesn't seem a very environmentally friendly thing to do. I thought Toby was supposed to be an eco-warrior."

"He's upset about his mother," Graham replied. "I read somewhere that grief can make people behave in all sorts of uncharacteristic ways. I suppose he's not thinking very logically. Hey! I thought we were going for a swim?"

I was leading him in the opposite direction – away from the pool and down the long drive towards the iron gates.

There were two armed police officers guarding the entrance but they barely noticed us approach. They carried on their conversation, which we caught snatches of as we got nearer.

"Poor Toby!" the policewoman said. Clearly she was as smitten with him as Mum was. "I feel sorry for the guy. It's tough, coming back to all this."

Her companion – a stocky, grumpy-looking cop – replied sarcastically, "Yeah, it's real hard coming back to a mansion that size. I wish I had luck that bad."

"I don't think he cares about the house," the policewoman said. "He told me he was going to sell it right after the funeral."

My eyebrows shot up. "That's not what he said to Mum just now," I muttered to Graham.

"Like I said, his mind must be addled with grief. He's not thinking straight," Graham defended him.

"Maybe. Or maybe he's just really good at telling people what they want to hear."

The policewoman continued. "Yeah. He wants to buy a chunk of rainforest. Protect it from the loggers. Use the money to do something useful, he said."

"The guy's a regular saint," scoffed the grumpy-looking cop.

"Give him a break, will you? He's nice. One of the good guys."

"A good guy? In Hollywood? We should have him stuffed and donated to the museum!"

"Excuse me," I said.

They both looked at us, slightly startled, as if we'd appeared out of thin air. "Hey! You're the gardener's kid, aren't you?" said the man. "What can we do for you?"

"Can we go out please? We want a walk."

"Sorry kids," replied the cop. "You've got to stay here. Lieutenant Weinburger's orders. He wants to keep you safe until we have Len Radstock locked up."

"Oh," I said. "OK. Well, we'll just go to the pool then."

I turned, but before we walked back up the drive I glanced over my shoulder at the road beyond the gates. There was the bend where Sylvia had braked for the raccoon. She'd done it so hard that tyre tracks still marked the surface.

My stomach gave an unexpected lurch. There was something significant: something I'd missed. What was it?

I started to walk, but instead of going along the drive I headed off sideways towards the shade of a copse of trees. Graham followed. When we got there we sat down, and I leant against the rough bark of a pine and closed my eyes. Graham said nothing.

I thought back to when we'd first arrived. I'd been

asleep in the car. Fast asleep, not even dreaming. Then when Sylvia braked I'd banged my head. The Sat Nav had kept spouting that address and she'd got really flustered trying to switch the thing off.

Then there was the raccoon. Mum hadn't seen it, but then she never seemed to see anything. Which was unusual, I thought, because generally speaking she is pretty observant. I hadn't spotted it either; neither had Graham. And even though Sylvia had told us the grounds were full of them, we'd only seen one last night when Sylvia had been killed.

Last night... In the dark... The bandit-masked creature blinking as if it didn't like the bright lights...

It hit me with the force of a bomb blast. "They're nocturnal!" I exclaimed.

"What are?" asked Graham.

"Raccoons!"

He shrugged. "I know."

"Why didn't you say so?" I demanded.

"You never asked," he replied.

I was up on my feet, pacing. "Mum didn't see that raccoon when Sylvia braked because *there wasn't one to see*! There couldn't have been, not in broad daylight, because they only come out at night. Sylvia lied. Why did she do that? Why did she brake so hard? There must have been some reason."

"I suppose what we have to consider is what it achieved," said Graham. "What was the end result of her actions?"

"OK. What happened? I woke up. Was that what Sylvia wanted? She was watching me really closely afterwards when we'd driven through the gates. Why?" The answer plopped into my head, clear and cool as a drop of iced water. "*So I'd get a good look at Len Radstock*. Which meant she already knew he was there!"

I thought back carefully over everything Sylvia had said and done since we'd arrived in America. "I was suspicious of her right from the start, but then she was killed. That was what confused me. Let's pretend for a minute that she didn't die."

"You don't think Sylvia might have been behind everything?"

"It's just a theory," I said. "Come on Graham, let's give it a go. Suppose Sylvia was the one who let Len Radstock in?"

"Why would she have done that?"

"Maybe it was so that he'd get the blame for everything. He looked really scared when I saw him. And upset too – not like he'd just deliberately killed his ex-wife in cold blood. Suppose Baby Sugarcandy was already dead by the time he showed up?"

"It's theoretically possible," agreed Graham.

I remembered something else. "There was that address, wasn't there – the one the Sat Nav kept blurting out? She didn't want us to hear that – she got really stressed over it. It was the only time I saw her flustered. I wish I could remember what it said."

"1171 Orangeblossom Boulevard," Graham answered promptly. "I made sure I remembered it. It's about a mile from here."

I was impressed. "How do you know that?"

"I paid close attention to the street names when Lieutenant Weinburger drove us back yesterday," Graham replied. "It's a habit, I suppose. But what does that address have to do with anything?"

"Well Sylvia organized our flights and everything, didn't she? If she was planning on framing Len for the murder maybe she was the one who invited him over here. Suppose she organized his flights too? She could have collected him from the airport and taken him to Orangeblossom Boulevard – that would be why the address was on the Sat Nav and why she was so bothered when it went bonkers like that. Then maybe she gave him a key to get in to the estate? It could have all been a set-up!"

Graham shook his head. "I agree that Sylvia could have killed Baby Sugarcandy and then gone off to collect us from the airport. But then when Judy died

Sylvia saw Len. He must have killed Judy."

"Not necessarily. No one else saw him, did they? We were right near there and we didn't. Not even my Mum saw him, and she was walking around on the terraces all morning. Suppose it was like the raccoon? Suppose none of us saw Len *because he wasn't there to see*? Sylvia could have taken the drink to Judy, lured her to the side of the pool and then strangled her. She'd said she was on her way *to* the pool, but she could just as easily have been coming *back*."

"I can see it could have happened like that." Graham was nodding like a toy dog on a car shelf. "But if that was the case, what was her motive?"

I chewed my lip. There had to be something! I remembered Sylvia's face on the night she'd died – that slick of lipstick, the dress, the radiant smile... And then I spoke aloud as an idea came to me. "Not some*thing*... Some*one*." She'd done it for someone. And her reward was to be killed by the very person she'd tried to please. *"Who benefits?"* I said slowly. "We asked that right at the beginning. There's only one answer to that. There always has been!" I balled my hands into fists and pressed them to my eyes in sudden fury. "How could I have been so *stupid*?"

Graham tried to catch up. "You mean it's not the puppeteer?"

"Oh, the murderer's a puppeteer all right. But it's not the Punch and Judy man," I snarled angrily. This killer didn't work with wooden dolls, but with real life human marionettes. "He's been treating everybody – including us – as if we're puppets. He's put us on a stage and got us dancing just the way he wants. He's been pulling our strings all along." I gritted my teeth when I saw how completely I'd been taken in: I'd played my part perfectly; I'd done exactly what he wanted. Well, not any more.

"I don't understand," said Graham. "Who…?"

"Toby," I growled.

Graham's eyes almost popped out of his head. "But he's so nice," he protested.

"No he's not. He's a very good actor. Don't you see? He's going to get the whole estate. He must have been planning this for years."

Graham paled. "So what do we do? Tell Lieutenant Weinburger?"

"No. It took enough time to persuade him it was the Punch and Judy man in the first place. It'll take too long to convince him it's Toby. We've got to get to Orangeblossom Boulevard right now."

"Why?"

"Because if we don't another murder will be committed!"

OVER THE WALL

I didn't like leaving Mum walking around Baby Sugarcandy's grounds with a murderer, believe me, but I didn't have much choice. If Toby knew that I'd worked out what he'd been up to we'd all be done for. Plus I knew from experience that once Mum started talking about gardens she'd be at it all morning. If we were lucky she'd keep Toby fully occupied while Graham and I:

a) found Len Radstock;
b) warned him he was in danger; and
c) persuaded Lieutenant Weinburger that Len Radstock had been framed.

But first we had to escape from the grounds. The

police cordon around Baby Sugarcandy's estate was there to stop the murderer from getting *in*. I reckoned they wouldn't be looking quite so hard for two kids getting *out*.

I could see the two cops on the gate were still talking. We crept along the boundary looking for an exit route. The wall was high, but if we could find a tree that was close enough we could use it to climb up and over. Just over the brow of the hill, out of sight of the cops, we found it – a slender, sloping pine with a branch that reached out across the wall. I started to scale the tree, arms and legs wrapped tightly around the trunk as if it were a thick rope. Once I reached the branch I clasped it and swung myself along, hand over hand, until I was dangling on the far side of the wall. The ground was about three metres below. It was a long drop, but I curled into a ball on impact and rolled sideways to soften the blow. I was dirty, but uninjured. Graham dropped down after me, white-faced and shaking, but doing his level best to keep up. The road to Baby's estate crossed the hill in zigzags but we went straight down, slipping and sliding over scree and stones, weaving between trees and bushes, until we reached the bottom. As soon as we were on level ground I began to run, my feet pounding hard on the dry earth, Graham staggering along a few paces behind.

I'm a good runner – I've won medals for it at school – but by the time we reached Orangeblossom Boulevard my heart was pounding so hard that it was bruising my ribs from the inside; my lungs were threatening to burst; and I had a stitch that was practically bending me double. Poor Graham looked as if he was about to die. We paused at the end of the street just long enough to recover.

"1171's over there," Graham wheezed.

"Right," I huffed back. "I'll go in and see if I can find Len Radstock. We need to get him out of there. You stick around out here. Keep an eye on the door, OK? If anything happens, shout for help."

I took a few deep breaths and calmed myself. Then I set off along the street. I reached 1171 and studied the door. The smart apartment block had fifteen buzzers in a column. None of them had the name "Radstock", but then that was hardly surprising.

How was I going to find him? Once more I read the list of names next to the buzzers. They were all neatly printed and perfectly legible apart from one. The flat at the top had a label that was scuffed and the ink had run so badly that the name couldn't be read by anyone: not pizza delivery guys, not the postman, not friends. Either it was empty, or whoever was staying there didn't expect any visitors. Following my hunch, I pressed the buzzer. No reply. I pressed it again. Nothing.

But then he wasn't going to answer, was he? For all he knew, I could be the police … or the murderer. I'd have to find another way of getting in.

I pressed the buzzer below and a voice barked through the intercom, "Yeah?"

It was nearly lunchtime. Worth a try. "Pizza delivery!" I yelled.

"I didn't order no pizza."

"Sorry, wrong buzzer."

A stream of rude words crackled back at me, making me wince. I tried the next one down.

This time the offer of food was rewarded with, "That was quick! Come on up."

There was a click from the lock as the person on the other end of the intercom pressed the button to release it. Pushing hard against the heavy front door, I slipped quietly into the building.

I opted for the lift, but it moved achingly slowly. I jiggled nervously on the spot as it rose through the levels, stopping at each one, finally pinging to a complete halt on the fifteenth floor.

This was it. I was here. I stepped into the narrow hallway. The stairs leading back down were to my right. Opposite me was the front door to the apartment Len Radstock was staying in. Or might be. I hoped I'd got it right. Swallowing nervously, I crossed the hall and knocked on the door. Not loud enough, I thought. I banged harder. No one came to answer, but I heard something inside – the faintest movement, as if someone had been startled, but had now frozen into silence. I banged again. Nothing.

So I cleared my throat and called, "Mr Radstock? My name's Poppy. You don't know me, but I think I can help."

There was definite movement now. I heard footsteps approaching on the other side of the door, but it still didn't open.

"Please, Mr Radstock," I tried again. "I know you didn't do it. Kill Miss Sugarcandy, I mean. You have to get out of there. You're in terrible danger."

No answer. Just the sound of someone's breathing – short and hard as if they'd had a shock.

"Let me in, Mr Radstock. I know who did it. I've worked it all out."

At last the door creaked open and a deep, warm, American voice drawled, "You do, huh? Like I said, you're one smart cookie."

And as I was seized by the arm and yanked inside my eyes widened with horror. Because the man who had answered the door wasn't Len Radstock.

It was Toby.

FIGHTING THE DEVIL

"YOU know what my mother used to say to me when I was a kid?" asked Toby calmly as he tied me to a chair. Len Radstock was lying on the floor nearby, his thinning hair crusted with scarlet. He wasn't moving. "'Toby,' she used to say, 'You're so sharp that one day you're going to cut yourself.' I never understood what she meant. I never thought it was possible for a person to be too smart. But then I met you, Poppy Fields, and now I get it. You're so sharp you're going to get yourself killed. Seems a pity when you were doing so well on my behalf, but there you go."

"How did you get here before me?" I demanded, desperately playing for time.

"I could see from your face you weren't planning to go for a swim. I figured you might work it out. So I made my excuses to your mother and drove straight here to finish the job. And now I'm almost through."

"You don't need to kill me," I protested.

"Oh yes, I do," said Toby. "Because if I don't you'll go blabbing to the police, I'll get arrested and the whole beautiful plan will crumble into nothing. And I can't allow that, Poppy, really I can't. I've been working on this too long to see it fall apart now."

"Was Sylvia part of the plan?" I asked. "You knew her, didn't you? You were lying when you said you'd never met her."

"Sylvia! What a sweetheart! She was so obliging: believed everything I told her so easily. She went off to work for my mother without a murmur just so I could keep an eye on Judy. You see, when my dear little sister moved back in and started spending my mother's money I knew she had to go. And then I thought, well, why not kill them both? But I couldn't see a way to do it. Not until Len wrote that cute little note to my mother saying he still loved her, and could they start over? I wasn't going to allow her to squander her fortune on some old guy. But it worked out real well in the end. As soon as Sylvia told me he was a Punch and Judy man, I knew I had the perfect fall guy. She made all the arrangements for him to come and see my mother. Heck, she even booked this apartment for him to stay in. If there's one thing I can say about Sylvia it's that she was efficient."

"So why kill her? She thought you two were getting married."

He laughed cruelly. "Like I said, she was gullible. She'd outlived her usefulness. And I think I can manage to find someone more attractive than Sylvia, don't you? A model. An actress. An heiress, maybe. Especially now I've got millions of dollars to my name."

"But how did you get into the grounds?" I asked. "The place was crawling with police."

"Sweetie, I was raised there. I know every tree, every rock, every hiding place. It's easy to avoid attention if you know where you're going." He finished securing me to the chair and stood up. "That's enough shooting the breeze. It's been real nice talking to you, Poppy, but now I've got to get going. So long." He smiled his rich, warm smile and turned towards the door.

"Are you just going to leave me here?" I yelled.

"Well, yes. I have to go and comfort your geeky friend and your poor mother for the tragic loss of her daughter."

"You leave Mum and Graham alone!"

"No can do, Poppy. Sorry. You know, I have

something special planned for you. The finale to the whole show. It's a perfect ending, believe me."

My brain was working frantically, wondering what Toby meant. What did he have in mind? How was he going to finish me off? What was the last scene of the Punch and Judy show?

Before I could ask him anything, he was gone. Stepping over the corpse of Len Radstock, he walked up the narrow hallway. The front door slammed. There was silence. And I was left in an empty flat with a dead Punch and Judy man.

Panic rose in my chest like a great bubble, swelling into my throat and threatening to choke me. I had to get out of there!

I began to wriggle in the chair. I'd dimly remembered that old circus escapologist's trick and tensed my muscles when Toby tied me up. I relaxed and could feel the ropes slacken a little. But only a little. I sighed. Circus escapologists were big, brawny men with massive biceps. I didn't have enough muscles to give me the slack I needed.

Perhaps I could reach the door. If I leant forward I could edge the chair across the room. My ankles were tied to its legs, but if I wobbled from side to side I could probably make slow progress. Quite how I'd open the door when I got there I didn't know. I'd work that out later. But first there was the obstacle of Len Radstock's body blocking my way. How would I get across him?

I looked at his lifeless form, and a wave of pity and despair washed over me. I began to cry. "I'm sorry," I whispered. "I should have got here sooner."

"Not at all, my dear," a voice replied in a crisp English accent. "I would have said your entrance was perfectly timed."

Jaw dropping, I stared at the body. An open eye stared back at me. For a moment I couldn't decide which was worse: sharing a room with a corpse, or sharing it with a member of the living dead.

But then Len Radstock prised himself off the carpet, and I realized he wasn't a zombie. He was alive, unharmed and untying the knots that bound me.

"But…" I croaked. "How…?"

"We'll do explanations another time, shall we? I think first we'd better both get out of here, before the final curtain falls."

"But you're bleeding…"

"Ketchup," he said briefly. "I was eating a hot dog when Toby walloped me. I lay still, hoping he'd think I was a goner. Then you turned up and he didn't think to check whether I was still breathing."

When the last knot was untied we both ran for the door. As we reached it an image came into my head.

Mr Punch. The devil. A big fight. Punch winning – sending Satan back to hell in a puff of smoke.

It all flashed through my head a split second before a mobile phone rang, and the room was ripped apart by a violent explosion.

THE FLAMES OF HELL

THE blood was real this time, and Len's eyes wouldn't open no matter how loudly I yelled at him. We'd been thrown through the front door and across the hall by the force of the blast. Len had smashed his head on the metal lift doors and slid down, smearing a scarlet stain all the way to the floor. I'd been behind him, and he'd cushioned my fall, although my back had taken more of the blast. I could feel lacerations across it and on my legs. I knew I was injured, but at least I was conscious. It was up to me to get us both out.

The apartment behind us was ablaze and already flames were licking out of the front door and edging towards us.

I tried again. "Len! Mr Radstock! Can you hear me?" I screamed. "Wake up!"

He gave a faint groan, but that was all. I'd have to drag him.

I knew better than to use the lift. Graham had once told me that lifts stopped working in fires, and we'd be trapped inside like chickens in an oven. If we were going to escape it had to be by the stairs.

I took an arm and tugged, but he was so heavy; so awkwardly floppy. I couldn't shift him. Flames had reached the soles of his shoes and for a moment I was tempted to leave him – to run away and save my own skin. But if I left him to die, I'd be no better than Toby.

I bent down and tried again. Sliding my hands under his armpits I laced my fingers together across his chest and heaved. He moved. Just a fraction, but enough to give me hope. I tugged again and dragged him towards the stairs. Pulling for the third time, I tripped over something and fell backwards. Pain tore through me but I got up and yanked him away from the flames.

We were fifteen floors up. We'd never get down the stairs at this rate. The building would crumble before we were even halfway!

Then I noticed what I'd tripped over. The door to the flat. It had been blown off its hinges. If I could get

Len onto that it might be easier to move him.

I rolled the Punch and Judy man onto the smooth wood. Then I shoved it to the top of the stairs. The flames were roaring now, eating into the roof behind me. Timbers were crashing down, and I didn't have time to think. I gave a hard shove and gravity took over. The door – with the insensible Len Radstock lying, singed and bloody, on top of it – took off down the stairs like a bobsleigh.

Turning the corner was the difficult bit. When the door reached the end of the first flight of stairs it hit the wall with a sickening thud and Len crumpled like a concertina. I leapt down after him, thanking my lucky stars that I'd put him on the door feet first because otherwise it would have been his head that had hit the wall. Heaving the door around the corner I launched him once again, and waited for him to hit the wall below. Hoping desperately that the violent bumping and crunching wasn't going to kill him, I sped down.

We'd done three bone-shaking, exhausting flights of stairs when other tenants started appearing, fleeing for their lives with their most precious possessions clasped in their arms. I was so glad to see other living, breathing people that I could have wept. And when two of them dropped what they were carrying and picked Len up as if he was on a stretcher, tears of gratitude flowed down my sooty face. As we ran down the stairs there came the miraculous sound of sirens. Flashing blue lights bounced off the walls, and several burly firemen appeared through the smoke. Hoisting him over a shoulder, one took Len to safety. And then there was Graham – running *into* a burning building to find me – shouting, "I told the police! I saw Toby coming out and I phoned them. Are you OK?"

I managed to give Graham a reassuring smile as, just before I fell into unconsciousness, I was hoisted off the ground and carried from 1171 Orangeblossom Boulevard in the arms of the biggest fireman I'd ever seen.

TOBY'S GRAND PLAN

THE first thing I thought when I came round was "Ouch!" closely followed by, "Where's Graham?" and "Where's Len?" and then, frantically, "Where's Toby?"

I was on a bed, and my back was screaming with pain. I knew from the antiseptic smell and the faint beeping of medical machinery that I was in a hospital. When I opened my eyes, the blotchy face of my weeping mother slowly came into focus.

"Don't cry, I'm fine," I said, my voice sounding scratchy and dry.

"Thank God!" said Mum furiously. "How could you? What were you thinking, trying to get yourself killed like that?"

"Where's Toby?"

It was Graham that answered. "At the police station. Lieutenant Weinburger has taken him in for questioning."

I nodded. "Good."

"The lieutenant wants to talk to you," Mum told me. "As soon as you wake up, he said. There are things he needs to double-check."

"Fine," I replied. "Send him in. But first... Is Mr Radstock all right?"

"He's still out cold, but he'll pull through, apparently. I wish I understood what on earth's been going on."

When he came in to see me, Lieutenant Weinburger got straight to the point.

"OK, kid," he said. "Give me the full story."

I told him what had happened in the apartment, filling in the bits that Graham hadn't been able to tell him. "Who benefits? That's what we wondered," I finished. "And we had the answer all along. I just feel so stupid for not seeing it before."

"But you had it all worked out," said Mum, mystified. "The clues... The Punch and Judy show... I don't get it."

"It was a trick," I said. "I should have realized.

I mean, Baby Sugarcandy wasn't scared of Len Radstock like Toby said. She loved Punch and Judy – she had those red-and-white curtains; she was wearing that red-and-white sash on her dress. She called her daughter Judy, for heaven's sake! And her son Toby – that's the name of the Punch and Judy dog. You wouldn't do that if you wanted to wipe out the past. She must have told Toby about the show when he was little – that's why he knew so much about it." I heaved a deep sigh of regret. "There was always something wrong about those murders. I wish I'd spotted it earlier. If you really wanted to kill someone, why would you advertise it like that? You might as well wear a big flashing badge saying ARREST ME. The drowning in the toilet, the throwing down the stairs, the sausages and everything… It was all pointing a great big arrow at the murderer, only it was pointing in the wrong direction. And that's my fault. If I'd spotted it sooner, maybe Sylvia wouldn't have died."

"You can't blame yourself for that, kid," said Lieutenant Weinburger.

"But I do," I said. "I should have seen that they didn't quite add up. I mean, it's Punch's *baby* that goes down the toilet, not an old woman. And Judy is Punch's *wife* and she doesn't get strangled with sausages. She never even *meets* the crocodile! As for that policeman's helmet – well, Sylvia wasn't a policeman, was she? It just didn't fit with the proper show. A *real* Punch and Judy man wouldn't make those sorts of mistakes!"

"It wasn't your fault," said Lieutenant Weinburger.

"But it was," I protested. "The whole plan wouldn't have worked without me."

"Don't be silly, Poppy," said Mum. "How could you possibly be part of it?"

"Do you remember that photograph? The one at the Chelsea Flower Show?" I asked. Mum nodded. "Sylvia had drawn a circle around my head, hadn't she? Not yours. And she made sure I invited a friend along too. Toby wanted us over here, but it wasn't anything to do with the garden. For all we know Baby Sugarcandy didn't even know we were coming – it was Sylvia who made the arrangements, wasn't it?"

Mum nodded but didn't speak.

"The important thing as far as Toby was concerned was to get a couple of English kids over here – ones who would make the link between the weirdness of the murders and the Punch and Judy show. Graham and I were fed big obvious clues until it fell into place. They used us to frame Len Radstock. And then Toby planned to kill him before anyone could find out he was innocent. He triggered that great big explosion so it would look as though Len had topped himself as the grand finale to his murder spree."

"Can you convict Toby?" Mum demanded. "I mean, will you be able to find enough evidence?"

"Sure we will," the lieutenant said. "Arson. Attempted murder. That's not a bad beginning. We've got witnesses to that. As for the other murders, he'll have left a paper trail – receipts, letters, phone records. We'll do the ninety-nine per cent, kid." Suddenly, unexpectedly, he winked at me and grinned. "And my guess is that Sylvia would have told someone she was planning to marry him – her mother, perhaps, a sister, a friend. There'll be someone who can testify that they had a relationship. Some way, somehow, we'll get what we need to put him away for a very long time."

The next day I was well enough to get up, and Graham and I went to visit Len Radstock in his hospital bed. He was sitting bolt upright, wearing a pair of red-and-white striped pyjamas and reading *The Times*. As soon as he saw us, he folded his newspaper and extended an arm.

"I believe I owe you my life," he said, shaking my hand.

"I believe I owe you mine, too." I smiled back at him. "Thank you for untying me. I'm sorry I had to shove you down the stairs like that. Did it give you a very bad headache?"

"It was a bit of a bone-shaker, but don't you worry. I'm just glad to be alive." He looked down for a moment and then said quietly, "I only wish Biddy was too."

There was a long pause, and then Len said, "I followed her career, you know, watched all her films, bought all her records. I was so thrilled when she wrote back to me saying she wanted to see me. Of course I don't know now if it was really she who wrote the letter or if it was forged by that secretary of hers. It was Sylvia who arranged our meeting. I got myself spruced up, red buttonhole and everything just like I'd worn at our wedding. Sylvia had sent me a key so that I could let myself in. But when I got there I saw…" His voice dwindled to nothing. When he started speaking again it was in no more than a faint whisper. "I could see how she'd been killed. Wet hair … that smell of toilet cleaner. That dear, delicate creature destroyed! I knew then that I'd been set up. I just ran. Cowardly of me, I suppose, but I was terribly shocked. I'd been so desperate to see her once more, and then to lose her all over again! I came straight back to the apartment and wept. And when I saw that her daughter had been killed I knew I would be blamed for that too.

'The Punch and Judy murderer!' I knew whoever was doing it would eventually come for me. Frankly I was beyond caring."

"You know," I said carefully, "if it's any consolation I don't think Sylvia did forge that letter. I think Biddy did want to see you."

The hope in Len Radstock's face was heartbreaking. "Do you? It would mean so much to think she still cared."

"Yes," I continued. "She was wearing that red-and-white sash, wasn't she? She was all dressed up – like she was seeing someone really important. As if she was excited about it, and wanted to impress whoever it was. I thought she looked like she was about to step on to a red carpet."

"She did. She was so beautiful."

"Well, she did that for you. That bit was real."

"It would be a great comfort to know she thought fondly of me. I do hope you're right."

"I know I am." I handed him a crumpled photograph. "The police found this tucked beneath her pillow. She must have looked at it every night before she fell asleep."

Len Radstock didn't answer. He took the photograph, in which a youthful version of himself was standing on a sandy beach with his arm around a woman who was as pretty as a china doll. A radiant smile lit up Len's face like sunshine after a storm.

Graham and I crept quietly away. We could see that Len Radstock was lost in happy memories, and we didn't want to disturb him.

There's not much to add, really. We were allowed home on the next plane much to Mum's relief. We had to go back to the States when Toby's trial started and by then the police had managed to unearth a whole load of bad stuff about him. They discovered he hadn't been saving the South American rainforests at all – he'd been dealing in drugs and was involved in all kinds of organized crime. So what with my evidence, and Graham's and Len's and everything else they found out, they banged him up and practically threw away the key. And it seemed that all his scheming and plotting had been a total waste of time in any case. When they read Baby Sugarcandy's will they discovered that she'd changed it a couple of months before she'd died. It turned out that she'd left all her worldly goods to The Last Slapstick – a luxurious rest home for retired puppeteers.

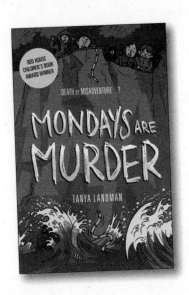

ZOMBIES? SPOOKS? OR JUST PLAIN MURDER?

My name is Poppy Fields. I never believed in
ghosts — until I stayed on a remote Scottish
island, and people started dropping dead all
over the place. Was a spirit taking revenge?
When Graham and I investigated, we began
to see right through it...

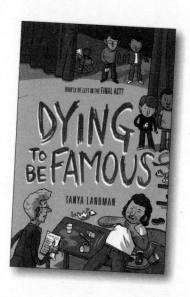

WHO'LL BE LEFT IN THE FINAL ACT?

DYING TO BE FAMOUS

TANYA LANDMAN

STAGE FRIGHT!

My name is Poppy Fields. When Graham and
I landed parts in a musical, we didn't expect real
drama. But then the star got a death threat and
the bodies started stacking up. Before we knew
it, we were at the top of the murderer's list...

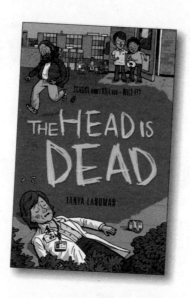

My name is Poppy Fields. When we
designed a murder mystery trail for
the school fayre, it was supposed to be a
bit of fun. But before long the head *was*
dead and Graham and I were hunting
down a real life killer.

ALSO AVAILABLE:

THE SCENT OF BLOOD / CERTAIN DEATH

POISON PEN / LOVE HIM TO DEATH

BLOOD HOUND / THE WILL TO LIVE

POPPY FIELDS IS ON THE CASE!